A FAMILY *in* SHAMBLES!

A FAMILY *in* SHAMBLES!

(Two Parts)

PHILAMA DUCTAN

Copyright © Philama Ductan.

All rights reserved. No part of this book may be reproduced in any form or by any electronic or mechanical means, including information storage and retrieval systems, without permission in writing from the publisher, except by reviewers, who may quote brief passages in a review.

ISBN: 978-1-64826-964-6 (Paperback Edition)
ISBN: 978-1-64826-967-7 (Hardcover Edition)
ISBN: 978-1-64826-948-6 (E-book Edition)

Some characters and events in this book are fictitious. Any similarity to real persons, living or dead, is coincidental and not intended by the author.

Book Ordering Information

Phone Number: 315 288-7939 ext. 1000 or 347-901-4920
Email: info@globalsummithouse.com
Global Summit House
www.globalsummithouse.com

Printed in the United States of America

Contents

Prologue vii

PART I

The Rise and Fall of Kitibel 3

PART II
THE CHILDREN IN SHAMBLES

Chapter 1:   Children Mourning 21
Chapter 2:   Briane under management 42
Chapter 3:   Bankruptcy 61
Chapter 4:   The Children in Shambles 83
Chapter 5:   Briane Moves Abroad 97
Chapter 6:   Reunion with Briane Abroad! 113
Chapter 7:   Education and Graduation 129
Chapter 8:   Home Return 140
Chapter 9:   Valparaizo's Renaissance and Wedding 152
Chapter 10: Prophecy Comes True 170

Glossary 187

PROLOGUE

This new version, "A Family in Shambles!" has been carefully adapted to replace the previous book entitled "Who Will Survive?" which you should have been acquainted with. The well-known phrases and metaphors are kept in addition to new characters, scenes, and imageries to direct you to the heart of the story.

Kootan was too young to convince Kitibel that voodoo was not the way to go. He had to wait until she died to persuade her daughter Briane, not to follow her Mom's footsteps. Eventually, a bond was created between the two in which Kootan proposes if Briane ever comes to terms with such bonded agreement, he will marry her but, under the two following conditions: first, Briane must reject voodoo's doctrine and second, join him in eradicating the same that is terrifying Hispaniola's Island.

Eventually, will Kootan keep his promise? And even Briane siblings, will they pay consequences for their Mom's act?

So, this version represents not only the family's story but also, the voodoo drama in Hispaniola's island, and in as much voodoo fascinates the couple and tapes their inquisitiveness to delve profoundly into it as youngsters, it will remain the cornerstone of the story. Death and tragedy will play such an important role to a point to ask, WHO WILL SURVIVE among four young siblings?

As for Kootan, even though the church has chastised him not to comingle with the voodoo's doctrine, he developed a special relationship with Briane's mom as a kanzo (voodoo practitioner); through her, he learned: mysteries, rites, ceremonies of the, and much more. But when Kitibel died at a river crossing, she called the voodoo gods, even God in heaven for help, and they closed their eyes, she swept away regardless.

Voodoo for Kootan, like it or not, seems to be the root of many good and bad of Hispaniola's Island. On the one hand, it represents laws and politics, medicine, education, agriculture, astronomy, family structure, and security against the foreign invasion; it also embodies death and deceit, despair and crime, hunger and poverty, and fetishes on the other hand. Actually, he thinks blaming voodoo for the Island's problem would be unfair because, the same folks who frequent voodoo at night to get even with enemy in counterpart, go to church during the day to receive the Holy Communion. Folks die of natural causes: atrocities, gunshots, hunger, escaping by the sea, and cataclysmic, etc.

Could this tragedy at the river crossing be an act of God instead of voodoos' work as rumors say?

Brace yourself for the following: culture, drama, history, and tragedy.

PART I

The Rise and Fall of Kitibel

I met Kitibel, or Kiti, as I liked to call her, when I was only seven years old. She has a daughter named Briane, who was born in the Dominican Republic, and because of our age similarity, I fell captivated by the family. But not only that, Kiti was also entrenched in a culture that had always peaked my interest, the culture of voodoo!

No one really knew when Kitibel moved to the neighborhood. The city register decided not to reveal her family identity to avoid reprisal because her father who's named Pepe, was deeply involved in the Haitian militia, which was a secret organization at the time. I grew up so close to these people that those who did not know me personally assumed I was a legitimate son of Kitibel. But it wasn't the case at all although secretly, I wished I were. So, once I was so thrilled to have them in my old town.

Pepe, was once a highly respected man in our city named Valparaizo city, located on the Dominican Republic coast of Haiti. The Haitian militia was run by a freedom fighter named Charlemagne Peralte whose aim was to outburst all the Americans from Haiti during the occupation of Hispaniola's Island. And after a swift victory by Peralte over the American forces in Haiti, Pepe then agreed to move to the Dominican Republic to continue the fight until final victory over the American forces. But Pepe remained in the DR for a long period of time because there was a pact signed between Peralte and Don Livorio. Unlike Pepe pursuing the same objective, the later was the head of the DR militia at the time.

To reach the Dominican Republic side, he and his comrades had to cross daily over Malpace River hoping to join Don Livorio forces to fight against the Americans'. He met one day a young Dominican lady who's named Lydia along the road; he fell in love with her, who became later Kiti's mother. And it took nearly two decades to free the nation and proclaim victory forever not only for the DR but, the entire Hispaniola's Island.

After the war was over, Pepe demanded Lydia in countless time to move to his city, Valparaizo Haiti with him but, Lydia refused. It was the case, many Dominicans believed that Haiti had nothing great to offer, they would avoid at all cost not to go there. But that was purely rumors and misconstrue. Lydia had never been to Haiti; then what's the ground for her judgement?

Valparaizo, Haiti's known as one of the greatest cities of Haiti; besides struggling for survival as was the case for many cities in the DR, amazing landmarks could be noted all over the place. The colonial houses which were built during the colonial period could be found few and far between. Many empty fortresses are erected at the summit of the mountain while tunnels built underground to camouflage the foreign troops. The City Hall is located at the center of the city, where people poured in to regulate all sorts of things. That was the Mayor's residence. Some beautiful parks at the confluence of the green mountains and rivers, and a gigantic cathedral named Immaculate at the main town square. That was the place reserved for the clergy. It was every local woman's dream to get married in Immaculate, the monstrous Cathedral, then travel to Port-Au-Prince for the honeymoon at Titanic Hotel. One of the oldest parishioners was Father Bon Enfant. This priest was a legend; he baptized almost half of that city resident before he passed away. Lydia was wrong but yet unconvinced. So, the remaining family: Pepe, Kitibel and Briane settled to Valparaizo city without Lydia.

Unfortunately, Kiti did not get to enjoy the best that Valparaizo had to offer. Shortly after the family newly established in that country, Kiti conceived three more children in deplorable condition: Enial, Witner, and Jack in addition to Briane, this dazzling girl whom I am proud to call my best friend.

Kiti moved to the populated area, which was essentially the livelihood of the entire population. The slum and poverty, crime, and despair marched like twin pair there. And I should be proud to state that I was the part integral of such place since I resided in that area as well. But the Hougans (male voodoo priest) and Mambos (female voodoo priest) lived in the side of the countryside to hide their ritualistic or sac-religious actions from the broader community.

Growing up, some of the prominent Hougans (voodoo priest) I interacted with were: Alcika, Docima, and Alanfer from time to time. But Alanfer was considered the most powerful and dangerous one of all and, I always feared him for that reason. It was rumored that he represented Lucifer in the flesh. Whenever I would travel far from town, I always prayed to God, not let me come across this man.

It wasn't uncommon for those who were struggling to make ends meet to take the chance to meet with Lucifer for a better life, and people always pointed figure at Alanfer as that guy. Ordinary citizens struggled through uncomfortable circumstances to go day by day with no hope of finding solutions to their suffering. So, those who didn't have the resources to leave Valparaizo in their desperation would turn to Alanfer. Even the politicians dabbled in voodoo.

"If the leaders don't pay their dues to Lucifer, someday Haiti will be destroyed either by earthquake or tornado. You watch!" predicted Kitibel.

The people who lived on the outskirts of the city were so poor that they would often starve to death during the winter due to food scarcity. It almost seemed as though the struggle brought a sense of comradery in the community. It was pleasant to observe how neighbors would share hot meals and loan cash to one other without judgment or prejudice. No one was left to starve because they had each other.

The citizens were deliberately sectarian. Injustice made them angry and violent. They were not afraid to make waves or be emotional about what upset them. They would go to hougan and mambo for guidance when something went wrong. Anything that appeared to threaten their routine would be considered unacceptable, thereby igniting a call for vigilance.

Many merchants, if not all, had to struggle to make a hand meet. In the opened market, no one, none, could proudly say, "I make enough money to make a living, no wonder to buy a home." They all had inspired to cook a decent meal on Sunday such as diridjondjon (rice with mushroom), toufe lambi (crunch with eggplant), banann fwi (fried plantain), and sos pwanwa (puree of black beans) followed by a glass of atomic juice (joined with a glass of fruit juice). Money was always scarce, even for nourishment. So, everybody struggled. Under this circumstance, a devil pact had been quite common, and for those who are not afraid would take chances. Why not Kitibel!

She woke up furiously and called Debora and Helena, her governors. "Deborah, you! Light up the charcoal and prepare breakfast for the kids. They must get ready by 7 AM to go to school." Kitibel said.

She sat down on a biott (a piece of 2 feet 8/8 wood) and began to hairstyle Briane. "What about you, have you done your homework? I don't want to hear your teacher, loudmouth…" Kitibel said.

"Yes, Mom!" Replied Briane.

Kiti bathed everyone. She mixed up various leaves, socked them in a ganmel (wooden bowl), and rested on her biott (a wooden 8/8). She rushed to the ogatwa (shrine) to begin her mazonzon (voodoo ritual). She spread the liquid overly with fragrances made of Florida's water, acacia, basil, basilic, amber, rose, vetiver, etc. She presented it to the four corners of the universe. She spilled it all over the children for protection before leaving the door. The governors included, "You need that for defense against the evil eye. It is also some good luck. You will be able to excel in this crazy world." Kiti intoned a melody to call all the Loas.

Kitibel continued with her wanga, mazonzon (voodoo ritual). She puffed the hefty grey fog of a six-inch Cuban cigar all around the living room where the family started the day. Briane seemed not to detest this behavior back then, even after this tragedy, because she told yesterday, she would like to replicate this practice. "Briane! You let Satan taking control over yourself too much." I suggested to her.

"This is the way it is." Responded Briane.

Kiti repeated the same ritual every Wednesdays and Saturdays at midnight sharp. She usually sent Helena and Deborah at dawn to the opened market to buy herself a rooster in addition to roasted corns mingling with peanuts, crude eggs, cassava, indigo, and numerous candle lights certainly. She would mix all in a layo (a flat basket made of dried leaves). She lifted all faced to the sunrise and called the Loas for assistance. Next, she would be transported momentarily to another dimension as she chants and performs various dances.

Secretly, I always thought these things would not end up well for this family. But for Briane, she thought that was fine. I felt like a lack of money or poverty was the problem. I decided to do something about it. I gifted my precious dog Cezin to assist her in her restaurant business. Thereafter, Kiti's restaurant was protected. She began to make some profit, perhaps just enough to save and win her daily bread. But, usually, people tended to go for more and more when they already tasted the feeling of lavishness or wealth. She now wanted a mansion in the city capital, move in the elite neighborhood in Valparaizo, a restaurant chain, marry in Immaculate, and certainly, send her kids to the best school in the capital and else. So! Kiti decided to relinquish her soul to Lucifer.

Kitibel got up. She pulled the biott and placed it underneath her grobounda (huge butt). She remained for a while in that way and bent her chin, rested it over her twisted palms, debriefing, "I am tired of being poor. I swear! I am going to change my life for the better. You watch!"

Kitibel hit the road to go and see Alcika, her prominent Hougan. He was known to be the family hougan. Everybody would go to him in time of need. But she was so embarrassed to go to him because of the purpose intended. Besides, she was afraid that her secret might be exposed because Alcika was a djolalele (charlatans). So, she decided to go to another one, the best in town who happened to be Papa Docima. She got dressed at an ungodly hour and paid a surprise visit to Papa Do, hoping to find an allez-mieux (a better life).

"What brings you here so early, Mom?" Docimas asked.

"I want some good luck, Papa Do. You know what I mean." She paused, "Since I lost Deborah, one of my servants even before, I've been doing poorly in the business, you know. I don't want to experience so much poverty. I am ready, willing to do anything to avoid it." Kiti paused.

"I am a Ginin's man, I don't work for money. This time with some bwa cochon, candle lights, Florida, and three pennies, I will see... You know..." Docima injected.

One day later, Kiti showed up around the same time. She presented with a basket filled up with the ingredients as proposed per Papa Do. "There you go Papa Do!" She debriefed.

Docima sipped some bwa cochon. He glared at her and grinned,

"This case surpasses my competence, but I know a grandmaster that can help you. His name is Alanfer. If you agree, I am ready willing to take you so far to Kenskoff to meet him."

"Alanfer, Lucifer! Beside Kenskoff is located on the far west Papa Do... It is too far away Papa..."

"Yes!" Responded Docima.

"Beside Spirits speak...nothing I can do, Mom! And this is a secret between us."

"How much, you think he'll take for his service?" inquired Kitibel.

"No! He needs neither your money nor your service. He is so wealthy. Instead, he gives away money to those who want some, but with some condition."

"Under what condition?" asked Kiti.

"As you know... do you deny that Lucifer exists?" questioned Docima.

"Positively, yes!" replied Kitibel.

"Truly, he is the most powerful being on earth after God. But the tricky part with him, he does not operate without retribution. He is the only one who knows what he wants. Even Alanfer...He is not the one that is making decision. He just represents Lucifer. He operates by command. He has a pack signed with Lucifer, the sole owner of that unbreakable pack." Docima paused.

"Sooner, you are going to meet with him. He'll tell you what he wants in your case."

"What about you... how can you save me, Papa Do?" implored Kitibel.

"Lucifer has no friend, Baby! While I worship the Loas, Alanfer serves Lucifer. The voodoo gods or Loas are less powerful, but they can do a lot of good things for people, such as healing, protecting the family against evil eyes (Lucifer's temptation). If you can get yourself a particularly good Ginin man, but if you get a pickpocket or dishonorable bocor who relies only on Fetiches, must of them are petro loas. They are not honest like my ginin loas originated Alkebulan(Africa)."

"This is what I do. I do not give money like Lucifer does. But Mama Alkebulan equipped me with what I need to know to save God's people." Docima said no more.

"In this case, do I have to pay you for brokering the transaction between Lucifer and me?" Kiti said.

"Not at all! You do not need to… I just help humanity. Got it, mom?"

"Deal!" clinched Kitibel.

Life was unstable for Kitibel. She was becoming more astute and stubborn every day. Her voice grew weak. It was as if she had been rebuilding her life from scratch, quite annoying at her age. Painful memories, indeed! The trip lasted four hours to reach Alanfer's doorstep.

Docima knocked and knocked! Alanfer popped out, "What brings you over here at this time? Any good news, Papa Do?"

"Let me introduce you to my friend Kitibel. She comes to request a favor hoping she'll be granted with it if she qualifies!" bawled Docima.

Alanfer bounced back and forth, howled, "Talk to me, Madam! What's the urgency?"

Docima stepped aside. Kitibel berated, "I had lost my key person in my restaurant's business. Everything suddenly went bad to worse. I want to find a way to bounce back immediately."

Alanfer, who is enjoying the fresh taste of a Cuban cigar, has suddenly shown some interest.

"My lady! In this place, we operate under the draconian rule. If you agree to my demand, you go home, your problem has solved just the way you want it to be..." then he paused.

"Now, I promise you happiness, not the way I want it, but your way. You will get all you want, to go by every day," he added. "If you agree to make a deal with me, list every person who lives with you in a piece of paper...even an animal. I will decide after all."

Kitibel pricked, "Yes, your honor!"

After a while, she handed the following names to Alanfer, Briane, Enial, Jack, Witner (children), Helena (domestic), and Cezin (dog).

Alanfer glared at Kitibel, "It ought to be one of your kids or yourself. You will have at least two full years to enjoy the wealth. At the end of the term, I will come and get the lamb myself according to the term."

Kitibel stooped, "How about if I give you a healthy young boy named Alcika? I love him like my son. Would you accept?" Alanfer paused and bellowed for a while.

"Did you get what I said, Madam? This is no joke! The person must be blood-related to you, meaning only your sons or daughters can be accepted."

While Alanfer shrugged to leave, Kitibel ponded, "In this case, I agree to sacrifice myself, Grandmaster."

To get to Kenskoff, it took them four hours, but to come back, the trip lasted a cool lifetime for Kitibel. But truly, some light appeared to be brighter for her at the end of the tunnel.

One week later, young men who had no crush on her would not hesitate to stop at "Chez Kiti" to admire her. This meant more money for Kitibel. She was embarrassed about her false teeth, and now she had a new one. A nightmare ended in the biggest asthma attack she had ever had. Life was unstable. She was becoming more astute and stubborn every day. Her voice grew weak. It was as if she had been rebuilding her life from scratch, quite annoying at her age. Painful memories, indeed!

Surprisingly in her routine visit to Kitibel to chat a bit about Briane's progress card at school, Kitibel always wanted to know about her progress in school as a godmother and mentor. That day Kitibel passed by the Lotto's place to test her luck. She just bought herself a ticket. The day after, it was announced in the air that the number came out as the first prize winner.

"What a lucky dude!" That was the theme of that day in a city where people had never seen someone with such luck.

As for Kiti, children, and entourage, "No time to think about otherwise! 'Laissez rouler le bon temps,' (enjoy life)."

Now, Kiti had owned one of the most expensive homes in Valparaizo, as well as a five-star restaurant. She invested in a new home in addition to a chain of five-star restaurants. The rest of the money was put in the bank as lifetime security for her posterity. But despite her newly acquired wealth, she was unhappy.

Kitibel regretted Debora was not alive to participate in the newly acquired wealth. She began to plan to travel around the world and move the kids to the capital. She is after a new miracle. Who else would she consult other than Turenne?

Kitibel frivolously woke up that morning. Her first customer for the day was the mayor.

"Helena, hurry up. The mayor is here."

The mayor ate fast and offered some excuse to leave. "I am meeting some government officials. I must go."

"I know you're a married man, but even though you're powerful, I deserve respect," Kiti reminded him.

Turenne hissed, "Hurry up! Talk to me, Kiti."

"Will you please help me relocate the kids to the capital?"

"I mean immediately. The kids must find schools before September, which is around the corner. Housing, as you know, is not a problem. They will occupy my newly acquired mansion," thought Kiti. Three months later. Turenne, the mayor managed to please Kiti accordingly. Kids had moved to the capital, great and exquisite schools were found, and protocols. Things seemed to be going fine. But not five years later.

Even though she was making a load of money with her assets in addition to a trip abroad with Turenne, she yet felt very lonely. She missed her kids. At dawn often, she always perceived an eye tracing her. She also heard steps tiptoed behind her. What she felt very strange, a tremendous black owl often encircled time her residence air space. That was now still drizzling and completely dark, and the musty smell of damp and the chuckle of the water as it ran down the street. Apart from making her restless at night and since she resided all alone having only Cezin for company, she yet felt very unsecured. Debora had been expired. Helena, her only governor, had to keep the kids' company in the capital. Decidedly, she sold all her assets in the city and hit the road to join the remaining family in the capital. The trip.

Kitibel arrived late at the bus stop with three suitcases. The truck was scheduled to leave at five o'clock in the morning, but it now was past six. She looked around in awe, refused to take any assistance, and the trip meant a lot to her. There had been a thunderstorm the night before, and the heavy wind blowing in her face and the possibility that her head might fall forward onto the pavement, she kept covering her hair, which was soaking wet. Invoking a loa at this time would seem a little absurd and useless, so she abandoned all notion of prayer, hid her discomfort, and focused on getting to her destination safely.

Kitibel took one last look at Cezin, while others were boarding. Kitibel perceived the same owl that she often spotted time at her space.

"This owl is up to no good," hissed Kitibel.

The driver was putting away a backpack that belonged to a handicap when it suddenly cracked open, spilling out a pile of pottery lasses, aprons, fake hair, and cheap old shoes.

"What's up with this dog," Kitibel shouted, pointing at Cezin.

"You have to stay. You always follow me. There's no room for you in my new home," she intoned.

Kitibel had agonized over her decision to leave him behind. But circumstances dictated her future and that of

Cezin. She turned to the driver. "Let's get going before the bad weather hits."

The driver knew that a hard rain meant the narrow, dusty road to the capital would quickly devolve into sticky mud. It had always been like that, but that was the least of Kitibel's worries. What she feared most was the river. That stream, when overflowing, would drown an eighteen-wheeler. This bus was much smaller. Its shock absorbers were visibly weak, its tires are bald, faulty backlights, and not strong enough to sustain the heavy winds. She realized she might have touched a sore spot, so she kept quiet.

"Are we leaving now?" Kitibel asked to change the conversation.

Despite the poor visibility and ceaseless thunder, the bus did reach L'Acul River, which was abundantly overflowing. The bus stopped abruptly.

"What are you doing?" Kitibel asked.

"Can't do anything but wait," he replied with consternation.

Sensing danger, the passengers began to pray. "Here, where are the spirits that I served: Papa Legba, Agwe Aroyo, and Danballah?. We are in your hands. Please! Help us..."

There was something else going on too. Some passengers were blaming the driver for having succumbed to Kitibel's request. Their breathing was audible, and their anger spread across their faces.

He was saying something else, something quite different from everyone else. He was invoking his own set of beliefs and gods. A scary look on his eyes, he seemed to be awaiting a blow. He knew their fears, their transgressions, their stories, and how they sometimes looked for a culprit or blamed the innocent.

"Yes, Papa Legba, master of the crossroads, Danballa and Aida Wedo, the serpent of Voodoo, I request your assistance."

Kitibel looked dumbfounded. She wanted to know what the hell he could say since he knew they were facing danger.

After everything was said and done, he proceeded. Halfway through, an owl perhaps the same one that Kitibel spotted previously flapped his wings.

"Go away, you moron," Kitibel shouted.

What happened next was too much to bear. The owl blurred the driver's vision, the engine failed, and the bus plunged into the river. Everyone drowned but Destiney to recount the ordeal.

PART II

The Children in Shambles

Who Will Survive?

Kootan promises to
marry Briane if she renounces to the voodoo.

Chapter I

Children Mourning

The first time I met Briane, she became everything I ever wanted. I never had a sister even other brothers to play with on the playground, and even though I was on my seventh birthday, I always anticipated, by the grace of God, our relation would remain until the end. But my values would never allow it because of our different beliefs. Her family worshiped the voodoo gods and mine Christianity. But this did not deter me from becoming a fixture in her family. And there are other reasons to be attached to the family.

Kiti sometimes called me my son and her actual sons: Jack, Witner, Enial, big Bro. But I never saw myself as such as they spilled around; the truth is, I had a crush on Briane. She tended to make me feel so special by always attracting me toward her. I never understand why I was the one she chose to hang out with. I even thought, in some way that I probably reminded her one of her peers back home when she used to leave in Santo Domingo. But as close I was to the family, Kitibel passed away, no one, not even Briane, informed me about it.

Anyhow, that's fantastic to me because it would have been too hard for me to handle because I am too sensitive as everyone know. But later on, I found out that what it was. They did not want to hit me with this sad news because they wanted to protect me by fear of depression or even trauma from my part.

Certainly, the distances and location of my residence was also a huge problem. In the monastery where I resided, my freedom was limited, even watching the news was a nightmare. Everyone anticipated being in bed at 10 PM, which basically left me no time to reach out with my friends and do homework. I really learned about the ordeal on my way to school in the morning when I bumped onto my friend, Colas. He passed it to me nonchalantly, anticipating I already knew about it. Then, he broke out in a hurry. Anyhow Kiti meant so much to me that I pretended, it could not be possible. "Maybe a fraudulent mistake?" I kept my calm.

She was so much gifted. She seemed like immortal. The exact time of her death was still unknown to me. Anyway, that was so sad to hear, hard to swallow, and painful to live with. Even though I had trouble coping with it, I finally understood the difference between the death of natural cause and that of supernatural as everybody was flirting around. I decided to rush to Briane's home.

She was at the front door when I got there. I greeted everyone with the expectation to make them feel how sorry I was and how much I had been missing them. I had not seen Witner, Enial, and Jack even Briane in weeks. They occupied a spacious colonial house in a great location, which their mom had mortgaged. It had seemed to be the best move for them, but it had also alarmed them in many ways. Now and then, they had felt the weight of the city upon their shoulders. They had found themselves in a town where most homeowners indulged in luxury. They had quietly managed to fit in and had done well in school. So far, so good! How about Briane?

Clearly, one month later, the ordeal was over. The clan returned to the city capital for schooling. Briane had since committed herself to be in charge as the oldest. Once upon the time, as she was getting ready to go out on a date, she found out that Enial had stolen money from her purse, but she had been tough with him for not doing homework. He quickly picked up a few bad vices since Kitibel relocated them to Port-au-Prince for better education. What Enial spent the money on got her really upset. He took his girlfriend to the movie theater. Briane obediently took him to the side and punished him. That must have been more humiliating than anything that had happened in the family. She was unhappy about Enial's sleight of hand, but she blamed no one.

Last time we spoke at the annual festival. We had talked about the hardship of the school's curriculum and how we had become savvy. Moreover, we had reminisced and thus found solace in doing so. We had grown up together but in the difference of reality of life. Boys and girls were not allowed to play together at a certain time during the day. In this case, we really had known each other but had never been close. It had not been by design but rather by circumstances of life. I had bumped into Jack a few times on a soccer field where my team and his had competed in the finals. I had also witnessed him bully his teammate; he had lost his temper often. He never missed the excitement, and many times he would be right in the middle of it as a shrewd instigator. Quick on his feet, that potato-sized boy would rather rush through the doors of a movie theater than buy a ticket, whether he could afford it or not. I had never invited him to my house. He had not seemed to care much about that either.

The time spent in Port-Au-Prince city was an adventure, it was quite different from Valparaizo's. Everything seemed to be in motion, moving fast, and everyone was part of the action. There were parties everywhere on weekends. Trucks polluted any areas deemed undesirable. Outbursts of gunfire were common. It was a lawless city. No one knew what the order was. It was anarchism, pure, and point-blank.

"Did Cezin die in the accident?" I pondered repeatedly. If he had, I sure would have been told about it. Under these circumstances, I dismissed anything which had to do with Kiti's death to relocate Cezin, "Kiti is not with us anymore. She's dead, but why don't I have the right to find out whether my dog is alive or dead as well?" I thought.

There were times I am convinced if Cezin had somehow managed to climb in the back of the truck, but again the cloudburst might have been too heavy. Other times, I thought he could have fought his way out of the river, swimming against the tide. He was smart enough to do that, and he was strong enough to do more than just that.

By that point, I was reckless. I could have asked Briane, but I was certain she would have been either evasive or told me something that made no sense. I was determined to know. I had made an inquiry to Witner, but he too had been in the dark, unable to reveal anything. Moreover, he had the nerve to order me to look for Cezin, and when I found him, I should bring him to his house. To him, Cezin belonged to his family—and that was that.

Despite being on herself, Briane surely was no longer the same person and suffered the most. Things turned around quickly soon after Helena had left to live with a much older man. Being the oldest, Briane was given the green light to be the primary caretaker. It was a tough decision she said she would never regret. Little did she know that she had no choice.

She courageously managed what her mom had left behind. Unfortunately, since Kitibel had not prepared a will, Briane did not know for sure what was left. Since then, Briane had been too busy to find time for herself. I found out about it later when I tried to flirt with her. She told me repeatedly that she had rarely gone out on a date, and if she had agreed to go to the movies with an interesting fellow, she would bring Witner along—just to be safe. And of course, Witner would inquire about anything that came to mind. That would frustrate her date. This boy would not keep his mouth shut. He was very protective of her and let everyone know that too. He was short, but he would wear boots—perfect for kicking hard. Perhaps he was acting out of fear. It was the inevitable fear in his eyes that was cruel and unchecked by reality. He had his load too, nonetheless. When Briane was out of town for a few days, Enial would take charge and bully Witner all day long.

Briane could rarely sleep well at night. It was not insomnia either. What was becoming of her? It was not clear to me at all. Was she unhappy? Was she traumatized about the loss of her mom, her absolute best friend, so to speak? Yes, she was. The reality was that she was too secretive. No one was able to penetrate the hard shell she covered herself with. She adhered to the unwritten code of womanhood as strictly as she knew how. She would not consider anything that would make her heart pound absurdly. Briane had bleached her hair, lost strands of it from a cheap perm, and wore a bandana to cover it. She sewed her own clothes. The skirt was always either too long or too short. She was beginning to look just like her mother. Her beauty and mannerisms made her quite exotic. Men would offer her a ride when she used to pick up Enial from school. The hell with them, she would say. She would not mind hopping on a *Tap Tap* (a minivan with wood benches that would take a lot of passengers from one slum to another). In fact, she would go as far as to pay an extra fee to sit in the front with Enial to avoid the charlatans in the back. They had bothered her many times before and made advances and reciting lines she did not think were humorous or clever.

Once, she told me the story of how a driver who was excitedly staring at her thighs almost rear-ended an ambulance. She screamed her lungs out before he slammed on the brake. It had been such a vivid memory. She would make no fuss about it now. In retrospect, she was pleased to have saved her life and those of the passengers.

The secret of her life thus carried false speculation, and it was entirely her fault. She could not be persuaded to do things she did not know about. Lately, she would have to be in a convulsed aberration if she were to talk about her emotion. It was a pleasure to listen to her rave about the mistreatment of children in public schools, and her lack of confidence in the whole system. It was even amusing to hear her talk about being a rebel.

When I learned she was still a virgin, I sincerely believed she was being selfish. She was sweet—too sweet for her own good. There could be no public backlash, as far as she was concerned. And I had admired her for that. Yet she bore a deep grudge for me. I could never understand why. Sometimes she would mock or tease me, though she dared not go too far.

There were days she would prefer not to think about her responsibility and routine or to talk about her love and desires. But that was one of those rare days when Briane was very personable.

In the backyard, she showed me the plants. Almost immediately, my mood lifted. I wished I could hold her hands.

"You used to talk about your days as a Boy Scout."

"Yeah, I remember those days," I responded.

"Why did you leave home when you were so young?" She asked while buttoning her white blouse up to her neck.

"I was unhappy. I was clinically depressed." I began to stutter. The words could hardly come out of my mouth. I could not take my eyes off her. I was on pins and needles but was hardly terrified. I could not think straight.

"What can you tell me about father Bonenfant?" She asked straightforwardly.

"Not much, Briane, except he was battling cancer. He had stopped running the Boy Scout group a few years back."

"Do you believe he's still alive?"

"I don't know. But if you really care to know, I can find out."

I looked at her, and I saw her toughen. I did not know what was going on with her, but there was one thing I was sure of, she was not mad at me.

"I went to the cathedral last month and asked. No one said anything. They walked away as soon as I mentioned his name."

"He must be old and retired."

"He can't possibly be that old. Are we talking about the same priest?" She asked as she looked straight into my eyes.

"There is one and only one Bonenfant. When he was a priest in our hometown, everyone knew him. I mean, back then, if you mentioned his name, you heard about all the good things he did and how compassionate he was." I said halfheartedly.

I did not know what I would have said next. But I remembered having asked Colas about Father Bonenfant, and he had answered rather half-jokingly that he had died on the trip with Kiti. Was our role model dead? If so, why hadn't I heard about it?

"No, that remained a secret Kootan. Do you know how perverse are those priests? He was on his way to the capital to make out with Kiti. As a result, both were killed in the accident." Colas said.

I froze and gazed at him for a few seconds. Then Colas gave up, "I was joking Kootan. Father Bonn would be the last person to exhibit such behavior and laughs about it."

"I hope to see him when I go to Valparaizo. I will tell you all about it when I return," I boasted rather confidently.

I proceeded thereafter to talk to Briane, she nodded. I felt crushed that she wanted to go back inside to be alone for a little while. I had never seen Briane act that way before. I thought she heard what Colas said about her mother. Not at all, she too was concerned about the dog.

Believe it or not, Cezin was still alive. Even after he had failed to board the truck and fell unconscious because of the smog emanating from the muffler, he did, in fact, manage to return to his shed. The pain he felt was unbearable, the atrocious stretch mark on his leg was evident, and the bleeding would not stop. It took him a while to get back to his senses. He could barely open his eyes, but he was aging gracefully. He was lonelier than ever, which was a sign that his days were getting shorter.

Not once in his life had he been so hurt and unable to retaliate. He had not planned it that way, but now he was forced to deal with mysterious circumstances of life. He was being looked upon with contempt and loathing. Did he really deserve that? Anyone who had ever come close to him would say no. But, again, nothing could be taken for granted in Valparaizo. The worst part was that no one cared about Cezin.

Cezin had not been provocative at all when the man who rented the house from Kitibel surprised Cezin from the back. The heavyset man, looking scared, kicked Cezin numerous times, grabbed him by his throat, and tossed him out onto the gravel road. He believed that the dog would not make it far and would die where no one would smell his corpse. And that was the opportunity for Cezin to getaway. Cezin was not welcome where he thought was home. So where could Cezin possibly go?

I was in a state of shock upon my return home. The town in which I grew up went through a drastic change. It was an obvious change that I could not stomach. The maple trees were cut down to their roots, and the mango trees stopped flourishing. Huts and shacks were replacing most of the corn and cane fields. The river and the lake were dry and uninviting. The birds migrated to a faraway city. I felt as if I had been beamed to a lifeless planet. Most of the kids I had befriended moved elsewhere, in search of a better life. And the bullies I had were now either dead or jailed. I had expected to see my cousin Sony. But he too had moved to Port-au-Prince.

It was about eight o'clock in the evening when I knocked at several times on the door of what used to be Kitibel's house. There was no answer. The door was ajar, so I peeked in. No one was home. I sure recognized the house, which was in a sorry state. I wanted to be convinced otherwise. It could not have been possible to turn his shed into a living space—but it was. Suddenly, I heard a pinch of moan emanating from the bushes behind the shed. I was attentive but a little scared. Could it be a dying animal? Yes, in fact, I was right. It was a dog in real pain. It was Cezin.

I could not rush him to the vet clinic because it had been closed and remained empty for years. But I had to do something. And whatever it was had to be done fast. I fed him but he took longer than usual to bite. He had lost his good-natured sense of smell, so I forgave him for not recognizing me. Somehow, he was grateful for me. Perhaps that was the first meal someone had offered him in a month. And possibly the last! I was just concerned about his survival.

A janitor whose name Fransic, and was on his way to work, stopped by.

"Have you any idea what happened to this dog?" I asked him.

"How would I know? I stopped messing with dogs the very day I joined the Baptist church. I am clean now."

"What a change!"

"You could say that again." He said, with pride.

"I must return to Port-au-Prince tomorrow. I have no room for him. Would you take him if I paid you?"

"I said I don't have anything to do with dogs."

"You won't harm him, I know." I added.

"How much are you giving me now?" He wanted to know.

I was relieved. I handed him a few gourdes. He agreed. I sobbed as I was holding Cezin. In my heart, I knew that his contempt for his environment had built. There was something about him I greatly admired: He feared no one and nothing, even injured. As a puppy, he would seem forever in the background. Those thoughts gave me hope during an icy realm of incredulity and anguish.

I patted him and put him on my shoulders before he left with Mr. Evil—turned—Christian. But I went to bed that night praying God to make Kiti's death natural instead of supernatural. I dreamt about all sorts of things because I knew Briane would ask me to coach her, and I would not know how to handle such situation.

"Is Lucifer tall or short, cute or ugly, human or monster, or simply, a gentleman?" Then, there she came.

She wanted my help just like I thought. But I advised her after a long conversation to reevaluate herself as the oldest and reject voodoo altogether. She also felt hurt when I advanced, "If you fail to quit the voodoo, more Kitibel will perish under the same condition as your mom." Unfortunately, she twisted the entire tête-à-tête.

"These gods have been protecting us since birth. How can you say that Kootan?" She would not stop lecturing me,

"Besides, you believe in Christianity, sciences, and technology like I do. But I also believe in Papa Legba,

Damballa, and Erzilie. They have always been there for us. Do not worry! We will be fine. In fact, will you please, promise me not to break your relationship with me?"

I responded, "If the sun shines so bright, it's because of you. How can I live without our exquisite relationship, my love?" I tried to dismiss her finally.

"My only hope is that someday, your heart even spirit will dictate you just how much suffering I am enduring because of your friendship with the spirits." She shouted, "Wait!"

She debriefed, "You just realized that Kootan?"

I responded, "Not at all…"

I kept thinking about how the accident occurred like Kiti were my own mom… I felt the need to give her, her own space like I needed mine. I retorted,

"You know what I believe in. I do not want to deal with Loas, no wonder Lucifer solves problems. All I can say for the moment is, get ready to reject once again every single spirit. If not Christianity, sciences and technology will be your best bet." I broke out.

Kiti died, she left plenty of money behind surely. But she also accumulated a lot of expenditures to be dealt with, four children, governors, friends, ransom for the Loas and bocors, taxes, mortgages, water, and electrical bills. But would Briane be able to manage so much? She barely made the age of adulthood. And I also thought overwhelming voodoo beliefs had been so much ingrained in her mindset, she would not be able to act any better. Briane was my friend before all. I could not be indifferent to her situation.

I always lived close to Briane since I was growing up. When she moved to the capital, her mansion happened to be located only a few miles from the monastery where I lived under father Baltazar's supervision. In fact, Isabel thought that it was not fair to me, so she managed to relocate me to the capital about the same time Kiti's gang moved to Port-au-Prince. If we had never been separated before, why now? I vowed to continue the same intimacy with Briane and eventually to her family.

Suddenly Kitibel clicked as thunderstorm in her mindset. She just traced back the scene of the accident.

"Throughout the trip on his account, the driver found some of the passengers annoying. A farmer, a store owner and a tradesman all needed favors, and all had advice to give. He had been listening to them for too long, and she wasn't going to bother with them anymore. The bus stopped abruptly. Kootan!" recounted Briane.

"That ought to be Lucifer in action, not the voodoo gods that I know Kootan..." lamented Briane. Her eyes filled of tears while the boys are refuged by the dining table discussing what kind of cars they are planning to drive.

"Talk to me, please say something mon amour (my love)!"

I replied, "No comment Briane. I was not present to a point to pass judgment." I supposed ma Cherie.

"What were you thinking? Did you know what the driver said Kootan?"

"Sensing danger, I could not do anything. All the passengers began to invoke the Loas, my mom included. We are in danger. My mom looked dumbfounded. She wanted to know what the hell he could possibly say since he knew they were facing danger. After everything was said and done, the driver proceeded. Halfway through, an owl flapped his wings. My Mom died." Just like that.

(That very same day I traveled so far to Valparaizo. I was worried sick about Cezin. Even though I gifted him to Kiti, he yet represented the center of my life. I confronted Briane about it, "About the sixty-six thousand dollars question Cherie, what had become to Cezin?" She just hissed her shoulder. I knew I had to make some move.

I travelled so far to Valparaizo and got there early in the afternoon. It was about eight o'clock in the evening when I knocked on the door of what used to be Kitibel's house. There was no answer. The door was ajar, so I peeked in. No one was home. I sure recognized the house, which was in a sorry state. I wanted to be convinced otherwise. It could not have been possible to turn his shed into a living space—but it was. Suddenly, I heard a pinch of moan emanating from the bushes behind the shed. I was attentive but a little scared. Could it be a dying animal? Yes, in fact, I was right. It was a dog in real pain. It was Cezin. I could not rush him to the vet clinic because it had been closed and remained empty for years. But I had to do something. And whatever it was had to be done fast. I fed him but he took longer than usual to bite. He had lost his good-natured sense of smell, so I forgave him for not recognizing me. Somehow, he was grateful for me. Perhaps that was the first meal someone had offered him in a month. And possibly the last! I was just concerned about his survival.

I took the animal over Isabel's place. I explained this quandary to her and took him to a veterinarian. But Isabel gave me room and board that night with Cezin. I knew she had no time for dog. I did not even attempt to ask if she was willing to take good care of him. Instead, I went so far to the parochial headquarter. I explained the situation to my previous mentor, Father Bonanfant. He sheltered the poor dog for me without even asking. I was so grateful to the father. I reaffirmed my conviction to him, to never give in to the voodoo. I will remember it for the rest of my life.

Father Bonanfant smiled and blessed and dismissed me to concentrate in his breviary. I was absent just for two days from the capital to Valparaizo. But when I returned, homework had been compiled to a point where I ask what I would do. Meanwhile, people put so much weight on this situation, which could paralyze the entire country.

I spent my teenage years adventuring and questioning about the voodoo. I did not believe I should give up so soon on my effort, but would Briane join me in that contest?

She refused to let this crime go unpunished. She went to look for a Bocor to revenge Kitibel, and where did she end up to? Alanfers'!

That day, she and Helena climbed up a knoll disdainfully in search for such vengeance and found nothing but cover-up, deceitfulness, and lie. Obviously, Alanfer denied everything. He guaranteed he had nothing to do with it. But he claimed her death was the result of a bad judgment and never disclosed why.

As for Turenne, so-called Briane's stepfather, he could not care less. He would not even think about it. He too yet remained the main suspect. He kept spreading words around, "Those who hit by the spear perish by the same." The boys, indeed, had been too young for this Catch-22. Yet, Valparaizonians wanted to know the truth.

Briane surely was at no point the same person. She suffered the most among the kids. While she committed to revenge her mom through voodoo, the boys preferred to arm themselves with firearms to shoot anything with two wings that resurfaced above their residence. But who reappeared at their doorstep so far at the capital? Don Pepe.

The gentleman knocked and knocked quite a few times, and finally, Helena went to open the door.

"Hallo children! You will never imagine who I am." Alleged Don Pepe.

"Can anyone see any resemblance to me?" Pepe said.

"At least one of you should say something. You should be able to see my physical trait to you."

Enial shouted, "That would be me." Jack said, "No, that's me." Witner stood there numbly. In unison, they all approached Pepe closer.

"Don't be afraid, I am your gran Pa, Kitibel's Dad," Pepe said.

Everybody was stunned. They exchanged some words while Briane pondered this question,

"Gran Pa, I heard you came to my mom's funeral. I appreciate it so much but, where had you been when she was alive?" The boys bellowed, "Yes gran Pa!"

Pepe bowed, "Allow me to explain what happened!" He sustained, "Kitibel left me at a young age to move with her Gran Ma in the city of Valparaizo. I was jailed in a place called Fort Dimanche for political reasons. Her Mom, Lydia, had died in Dominican Republic. Your gran Ma, in case you did not know it, was Dominican. I could not send Kitibel back there. Besides you Briane were born in Santo Domingo too. According to some people, Kitibel was living alone when she gave you birth in Valparaizo, you the boys," he paused.

"In fact, I was released from jail one week ago, just in time to make up the time I lost with my daughter but, look in what situation I found myself in." Pepe understood that he needed to find ways to make peace with these kids. He accomplished this task with no problem.

One week later, Briane popped the question at the dinner's table, "Gran Pa I am so sorry to ask you this question, what was the main reason you were thrown in jail for so many years? You are talking about twenty years plus; did you kill anybody?"

"Not at all," bellowed Pepe. "You are aware of Valparaizo's situation, slum, devastation, hunger, crime, voodoo, and else. I was a former soldier, political activist since I was a teenager. I wanted to do something for the country. Perhaps you thought about it too," said Pepe.

"I wanted to be at least the town's mayor. I was denounced by my good friend Turenne. And it was punished by death if one spoke badly about the country, so I did. I was arrested and sent to Fort Sunday to die or be abandoned. But I was lucky to be released last week," said Pepe. Helena was kind enough to prepare a special dinner for Don Pepe, and I was invited to join the party at the table. I felt I should let my voice heard. I cracked a joke.

"No wonder why you began the same career as the same age as your Gran Pa Briane. I know now where you got that gene." Don Pepe smiled. The mood had swapped in different tune. The kids forgot their grief. They felt more secure. Gran Pa had been around. There was no reason to be so scared.

One week later, Don Pepe already forgot the miasma that threw him to jail in the first place. He decided to travel to Valparaizo to visit some friends. Briane gave him some cash because there was plenty of money in hand. After two decades at Fort Dimanche, he came back penniless and fuming. Besides, he really had no time to be worried about Turenne who had caused him his lifetime in jail. But Pepe had used the cash instead to revenge Kitibel.

He traveled all the way to Valparaizo to get himself the best Bocor in town to vindicate his sole daughter. But as soon as Mayor Turenne saw him around, he was shocked and speechless and knew what to expect. He inhaled and exalted a fresh Haitian's cigar as usual. He spat on the trunk of the highest coconut tree where he took his daily refuge, "Hallo Don Pepe, how long have you been released?"

"In the name of Jehovah God, the Merciful, I was given a second chance to see sunshine again."

"Oh Yea…" shouted Turenne.

"I'd like to know who oversees Valparaizo, this jerk belongs to jail."

Now he began to play the same trick that had caused Pepe to go to jail in the first place. He framed him once again.

He fabricated a document and sent it to President Francis.

"Pepe was just released from Fort Dimanche (jail) he is up to no good. Last night, according to one of the detectives, he was initiating some kids in a riot to overthrow Francis Duval," alleged Turenne.

Two weeks later, Pepe was arrested and sent back to jail, importunely this time for life in the penitentiary, where he later died. But before he confronted Turenne, he was told that Alanfer happened to be the main suspect in Kitibel's death. So, Pepe managed to work out his own vengeance to hit that man.

Sunday morning at dawn, all the merchants had already gathered in street fair to sell their goods. At this early morning, a commotion deprecated below the Calvary mounting, "Mayor Turenne passed away."

According to a reliable source, he may have gulped down too much barbancourt and suffocated himself in the process. When Briane learned what happened to this strong man, she uttered, "I don't wish anything bad for anyone, but I'm convinced Kitibel's Loas have been retaliated."

Subsequently Briane spent an arm and a leg with Alanfer to have her gran Pa released. All efforts were nulls. She learned later that he died due to malnutrition and remorse.

Briane summoned me that Sunday to come and see her personally. Since we both had a crush on each other, I thought she wanted me to make out. When I got there, I realized I had guessed incorrectly. She was ill-fated just like a fox. At this point, I did not know how to handle the situation, I needed help. I was not going to let her handle them all alone. She really needed me.

"But you haven't said anything yet to me," I supposed ma Cherie (my love).

"I just lost my Mom, now my Gran Pa whom I just met for the first time, has gone. I wonder who will survive. I can't imagine me or any of my brothers to be the next," she paused.

"Maybe I should pay some ransom to the Loas. What do you think?" She inquired.

"Briane, you know what I do best since I was ten and you were eight years old, searching for the truth about the voodoo. Now, we all grow up even the boys, we are adults right now. To make the matter short, maybe I should continue to make my search on that subject if there was something in the voodoo even vengeance, I would have seen it besides killing for no cause. Paying ransom for what?"

Briane pondered, "What about the owl Kootan? Countless deaths and suspicious species that strike at night, tell me why?"

"What do not you switch our tete a tete, your mom's state for instance. This is really the main issue at the present time for you."

"Kootan! You are the man. You always thought what the best for me is." Briane acceded.

Chapter II

Briane under management

Briane inherited a lot of wealth and I, nothing. In fact, my sister Isabel had to struggle so hard to come up with my expenses because my Dad Pekles was jailed and died in prison. But in as much as I loved Briane to death, I truly wondered if I would be able to keep up with this relationship. She frequented top private school while I relied on governments to achieve my goal. With this contrast, she was able to meet the richest kids for acquaintances while I only met the middling ones. One of Briane's classmates, whose name is Kemal and of Christian value like mine, had become buddy with her.

They developed special relationship while I remained in gumshoe about it. That was my truth. She could not be blamed for anything. How many times did she bring her fragile and so vulnerable heart to me and I refused to step forward? No! I wanted to be a gentleman, obey the catholic teachings, even Isabel. "Briane has been Satan worshiper and I, a Christian. I am not committing myself to her." I thought.

Fairly true for God's sake, Kemal would not ever be qualified for Briane. Perhaps someone who is deeply enrooted in the voodoo to enlighten her, I believed my friend Mark would be a better choice. But I was afraid of neither Kemal nor Mark at all. I lived with it for three reasons. First, I perfectly knew the brand. Provided I was alive, she would not ever take anyone so seriously. Second, I wanted her to take contact with Christian kids hoping she would convert to Christianity. Third, Christian boy would not ever touch a girl unless he tied the knot with her. So, this relation was just experimental, I thought.

I genuinely wanted to help Briane, even to show that she had someone to rely on, eventually to fuse the so-called owl in her mindset. So, I thought learning some more of the voodoo's trade would help a lot. Mark would be a perfect choice.

While I was playing soccer in the school ground with him, I pinpointed under his uniform an epitaph that he concealed, "Damballah and Ida." I thought he would certainly teach me what I need to know about the voodoo. But not only would he eventually teach me all the hangout points as I had just moved in the city. What yet remained mystery to me is the epitaph. I questioned him, "What represents this epitaph my friend?"

Mark alleged, "Not so simple like you think. This is the greatest god among the Loas. He is my symbol of protection against the lougarou (bogy man), that means a lot to me." Since that was unknown to me, I continued,

"Where did you get it?"

"My Mom is a Mambo. Her name is Dolores, the best in town. Maybe I should take you to see her. She would explain to you better about that."

I thought about Isabel, "She told me not to confront any mambo or a bocor alone; I never knew why." I shouted anyhow,

"Deal! But can I take some of my friends with me?" I thought if Briane even Helena decides to learn new tricks that would be a great opportunity for them. It is up to them.

Mark kept his words to me. And when he attempted to dismiss me, I yelled, "Not yet! I must ask you if you know about some important places such as the slum where voodoo has been using widely."

"Yes! Okay Kootan! This is nothing but I promise I would pay a visit to them. That would be the best way to get to know them," bellowed Mark and began to lecture me.

"Carefour, this is the place where you will find the Guedees Loas. But get ready to digest their trivial languages when they come down from the poto-mitan (a center pole where the spirit comes down when opening of the ceremony)."

"I reside at Carefour. My Mom will celebrate Guedees sooner, you all are invited. You will meet with her." Mark pursued,

"Cite Soleil (Sunny town) has been another one but be careful! Good and bad mingle together. You know what I mean. You will learn everything you like to know." He mentioned finally at last and not the least, "Croix des bouquets."

Since we both liked to venture, we gathered everyone to go on a tour. But surely, we gathered Mark by our side. Even though we had a chaperon, Briane was still skeptical.

I counted how many times she told us to "be very careful." Ten. She took pains to remind us that Port-Au-Prince was not Valparaizo by any means. She was right about that on all counts. And I knew she was, but to be so exaggerated like she suggested, that prompted me to think of the good old days when my curiosity had reached its peak Valparaizo. I had faced the Loas all alone and dared even the Bocors.

"Yes, I remember you had seen the Loas in action. Now you are still alive. What can Briane lecture you about the slum and the Loas?" said Jack and asked me to dismiss her since she was talking about a town she had never been to. "But not only that, we had Mark to rely on," added Witner. Still Briane sounded rather not convincing.

"But almost everyday someone got killed there. You will be going to Cite Soleil (Sunny City) possibly to face more owls. Remember what happened just recently."

"Gee, it's not like we're moving there." Enial added.

"True, the murder rate is high, but Briane, that's because they're poor." I suggested.

"Kidnapping, looting, rape, do I need to say more?"

She was indeed going to say more but refrained as soon as Mark came in. She must have figured she was fighting a losing battle. And now it is worsened even more since Mark agreed to join us.

"I could not believe what I was hearing. You all should be ashamed of yourselves," added Mark, very agitated. Everyone yelled, "Okay."

Mark yelled, "Hey Helena! What's for dinner today?" "Nothing, before I even leave this place, I went to Croix Bossal to buy some meat. I came back empty handed. And don't ask me why."

"But why empty handed," said Mark.

Mrs Kitibel used to say, when going to the meat market, if the product looks red, not to buy it because it could be human meat. And that was the case for me today. So, we all should be vegetarians today."

Witner shouted, "You think we are a bunch of cows. Why do you suggest that? Maybe we should order lobsters, shrimps, or even fishes?

"Okay! It is a good idea baby. This thing did not occur to me," said Helena.

Briane interjected, "This really should not be the time to talk about food. Why don't we pray to god Grand Bois to guarantee us a safe return before anything else? Sincerely to tell you the truth, I don't even want to face the owl not even one more time."

"Briane! Father Bonenfant would recommend reading psalm ninety-one three times before leaving this place."

I shouted, "Witner get me a bible." "Hell no," said the boy and sustained. "Everybody get on board before I change my plan."

So, to calm the situation, I patted Briane on the shoulder and thus she began with her mazonzon (voodoo work). As soon as she closed her eyes and called the Loas to the poto-mitan most of the boys were gone. They sat in the car waiting for everyone. Mark did not quite understand what she was up to, questioned,

"Are we supposed to take off now? I came here just for that. Who will be the driver?" Enial replied, "Of course that would be me."

When we got to Sunny City, it was noon. The first thing that went through my mind was, oh boy, Briane was right. Driving by the police station, we saw a man being beaten and tortured because, the corporal told us that the prisoner had been caught stealing a watch. All the bruises and skid marks he got meant nothing.

Briane said, "Let us make a deal. I offer you two US dollars; would you agree to leave him alone and set him free?"

The corporal replied, "Okay Mom, deal!" Surely, she did and, the man was released.

We veered off right quickly and passed a landfill where teenagers gathered to challenge each other. They sat over a garbage pile that was as huge as Mount Everest. This was their only playground, unsafe or not. Two wooden poles clustered by pieces of cardboard and rag, that was a home. Suddenly, two thugs in shades walked past. We could tell who they were by the way they looked, the way they carried their guns on its holster, and the way they stared at us. They were the new breeds of terror, the wise guys not to mess with. Those ugly pimple-faced thugs were, in short, *Tonton Makout (special government forces)*. We did not acknowledge them, nor did they approach us. Once they were out of sight, we took a deep breath.

"What are doing here, Kootan?" We heard someone shouting. To my great surprise, it was Mark. I hardly recognized him at first. He gained a lot of weight since our days as boy scouts in Valparaizo.

"This is my first time here. You live around here?" I inquired.

"No! But I moved to the capital. I have been back to Valparaizo since grandma died three months ago." He said.

"I'm sorry to hear that." Kootan uttered, before he allowed the boys and Briane to greet Colas. It was hard for me to hear Colas talk about his late grandmother. I had not met her, but father Bonenfant had talked glowingly of her.

Her death had seemed to shatter his dream, and it had. He had quit school to work to help her grandmother pay the bills, suffered malaria, and spent months lying in bed. The kid who had inspired to become a gynecologist was now a vagabond."

"Where are you heading to?" I asked him.

"I'm looking for my niece. I thought she would be here playing but evidently not. Well, I must go. It was nice to see you again, Kootan. Nice to meet you guys," said Colas. I offered him a ride and he gladly accepted.

But he lived about two miles north in a shantytown called "*La Plaine.*" We took a scenic route and fell in love with what we saw. Tall coconut and mango trees were the town's mainstay. We felt like we were in heaven since no one came out to bother us. I was willing to climb a tree, just for the fun of it. Enial reiterated he would follow suit if I did. We stood under a giant tree enjoying the cool breeze when a huge snake crawled on Witner's shoes. Colas said, "Let's get out of here."

"Come on, bunch of cowards. It's not venomous." I boasted.

"Ah, what you don't know is, when you see one, there might be a million other ones in the vicinity," he said forcefully. "So, you'd better listen to me if you want to leave here safe and sound."

Yes, we listened. We were now by the creek when a flame busted skyward. Something was on fire. It had to be. And right in the middle of a sugar field? We found a young woman and her two kids entrapped. She set the fire to prevent the snakes from coming closer to her kids, to prevent her from yelling and screaming.

Mark and I had enough of this. We began to hit snakes with rocks, tree branches, and with anything we could find. Meanwhile, Enial and Witner rushed her and the kids out of there.

She thanked us and, if that was not enough, offered us her last fruit basket. We felt it was unnecessary, so we paid for it and headed back. We learned that life was no plaything, and nothing could outdo good will. Perhaps it was her faith, perhaps not.

"Where do we go now?" Colas asked, as if he had a plan.

I personally did not want Colas to take control of the situation because we already had Mark who was a son of Port-Au-Prince. He knew the environment more than anyone else, therefore, I directed Mark to direct as we intended, "Mark! You know you had been selected to be our guidance. I believe you did not mind having Colas with us. He has been our friend since grammar school. We just happened to meet with him accidentally. Is it okay?" Mark said, "Why not? Let us keep going, so many to see ahead."

"I want to go back home." Witner suddenly plashed.

"I'm not ready to return home yet." Enial answered. "And I believe Kootan and Briane want to do something else."

Did I? It was hard to tell. I could be convinced to go somewhere else, indeed. But for now, something else was racing through my mind.

Briane implied, "I will not rest until I'm really sure what the owl is about."

"Where were the voodoo gods when my Mom needed them most? Not one goddess came to her rescue. Evil spirits did not seem to like kids, after all. Even Debora found no protection," said Witner. But when Colas heard all of that, he decided not to continue the trip with us. Maybe he did not want to commit himself too much as a previous boy scout, "Guys! I believe you really need to drop me home at Laplaine before you go further. I have some tasks to be fulfilled." We all agreed to it and dropped him home as planned.

But Mark had lectured me so much about what he saw. I began to wonder if the hougans and mambos failed to do their task or lied blatantly about the power of the spirits. I questioned everything he told me, spirits could kill a man and later bring him back to life as a zombie after his burial and a zombie could be laboring on plantations for years before neighbors knew about it. "Mark, what else is going on around here?" I asked him.

"What you see is what you get, my friend." He said.

"This place needs a lot of help. That's why I'm going to become an engineer." I said, looking at Enial's reaction.

"Well, that's all good. But I would like to remind you this is a farming area. It's not as flourishing as it used to be." Mark said, in a challenging tone. And he was right.

"Yeah but look at the roads." Enial added, with a sigh of relief.

"What about them? They are all the same everywhere I go. Fixed one day, broken the next." Mark countered.

"Maybe there are too many evil spirits around here!" I said, half-jokingly. Then Briane popped out the question, "Did you ever see an owl in the sky around here Mark?"

"Never," said Mark. "Beside the regular one which has nothing to do with bad spirits, but" he continued, "It can happen, I always hear my Mom talking about such a thing. So, to speak," groaned Mark.

"If you guys don't mind sticking around, I can take you where the real thing is popping right now."

I assumed Mark needed a ride to his mother's house and that was his trick to get us to drive him.

"They're playing music over there. If that is the case, what are we still doing here?" Enial inquired. He was apparently more than that, ready to go. And so, we did because our mission was to search the existence of that owl hoping to crack on real peace someday. *Carrefour.*

Mark was right and wrong on both counts. He took us to his mother's home where a voodoo ceremony was about to start. In a large room adjacent to the house, folks waited patiently and greeted us amicably. Every kind of food dish that was needed had been prepared the day before. I had never witnessed something like this before, young and adults sharing their mutual respect. This wasn't going to be just any type of ceremony, I sensed my impression was that this was going to continue until dawn and that Witner, who was already having issues with Enial and Jack over the use of alcohol, would not be able to hang around.

Although Mark's mom was busy bossing some guests around, she gave me an ear when I approached her diligently.

"I'm new to this. Do you mind telling me what's going to happen next?" I asked her.

"Keep your eyes open, young man. You'll see for yourself." She said, smiling.

"I sure will. It seems like it's going to be fun to watch." I replied.

"Is it your first time in a voodoo's ceremony namely Guedee?" She asked bluntly. Briane and I said, "Yes, Mom!" I just stayed freeze motionless next to Briane. She immediately understood she should let me do the talking.

"Well! I don't know what Guedee is." I added, truthfully.

Why did I ask? There was much to say. She did not know where to begin. She figured it would take a while for a naïve person like me to fully grasp what the heck this was all about. I followed her into the reception area where the drummers drank and smoked. I was not going to ruin her evening. She had me put stuff away.

"Let me put it like this. Guedee is just a Loa or voodoo's spirit. It is the most vulgar than the other Loas. The possessors express only in unrefined or trivial language. Do you get it boy?" Briane began to raise her voice, "Yes! I get it, but what about the owl in voodoo?" I said to Dolores, "Not so quick my dear. I think Guedee is completely different. We need to pursue our search further."

For me, I thought at first, she was stuttering until I realized she was munching on some baked peanuts. Then she squeezed my hands and leaned toward Briane while the boys for the most part could care less.

"There's Aizan, the one that protects us when you're on the road. Nibo, protects us from local foes. He works in consultation with Legba Atibon, god of the gate. You start a ceremony by invoking Legba. You want to know why? If you do not do that, no real Guedee will show up. You'll be wasting time and money."

She pointed at a gargantuan pole where Lega would soon climb down. The pole (called *potomitan*) was the support beam of the room and it also signified the roots of evil.

Suddenly, an alcoholic drummer was in a trance. He was now under the influence of *Damballah's spirit.* Interesting, I thought. Then his girlfriend was too possessed by *Aida Wedo.* This is a female spirit known as Damballah's wife. That was even more interesting.

She explained that *Damballah* was the most powerful among the gods. "He was present when the ceremony was about to begin. He came with Aida Wedo. You will see how they both crawl like snakes." She professed.

Two teenagers who came with their parents had jumped on Aida's lap. Two adult couples acted like two huge snakes, huh? They stood up; hugged people one by one. They leaned on the floor and began to crawl from one room to the next. They ate crude egg and cornstarch. After a while, the kids returned to their senses and so are the adults as if nothing had happened.

Dolores talked about the Guedee, *Brave*, who would act as a pig. Brave is a tough character, strong and belligerent.

"Some of them you won't see tonight." She told me. Briane who had the impression maybe she could find an answer to her problem from one of those Loas creaked,

"Why not? Why can't they be here?"

"You won't see these famous Loas today, Aizan, Legba, Agwe, Papa Zaka, and Grand Bois Ife. Each one serves a purpose on earth. This is not their assignment, what they were sent for on this planet." Dolores guaranteed what she alleged, and that was that.

"Where are the Loas presently mom?" questioned Briane, brimming with air of innocence.

"Simply in their own space or dimension," she said, and then paused. "For instances, Baron Cemetery resides in the cemetery. Grand Bois Ife lives in the bush. Agwe resides in the water, etc."

If I had not been confused before, I sure was now. Yes, that was certainly it. I had heard about this character named Baron of Cemetery and seen folks dressed like him.

"Baron...what does he do?" I asked.

"He's the chief, the absolute power. That is a big job, you know. And you do not just call yourself baron. To be a baron, you must be the first one to be buried in a cemetery. That is what gives you power over all the other spirits or dead people that came to be buried in the same cemetery after you. First means something magical. Nobody knows how. It is all a mystery. Rather you should ask why one attributes so much importance to January first. "About that," she inquired. Briane responded, "Oh Yes! Maybe you have a point." "You can't just go and get a zombie without Baron's approval." She dismissed us to attend other guesses.

Meanwhile, Witner, burning with impatience, began to pace up back and forth. He just gulped down the last sip of the teapot and implored that we should leave immediately. Mark did not think so, since it was right about the time when amazing things would unfold. And so now we were just watching. Young women lifted their skirts, their eyes and sex organ bathed in hot sauce, their face expressionless and their language racy, sexy.

Guedee, as I just learned, meant power, achievement, and invincibility. Baron, I had no firm idea.

Witner was standing next to me when he sobbed.

"I don't trust these people. They probably put more curse on us. If we had one owl to spot us, now, we will probably have two. Right now, I don't even feel good."

"Shut up, you scary cat." I blurted out. Mark said, "It's okay, Kootan. I believe that was my fault." Witner did not stop expressing his feeling seeming denying the purpose of the visit.

"You can call me that as you wish but I have a feeling someone's going die in here. And" he continued, "I am certainly sure, it won't be me."

I decided irritably not to make a fuss about all of that. I have my reputation to protect at school, first and foremost, my friendship with Mark. I decided to restrain myself and choose quitting over observation on this fabulous Guedees night instead.

We were standing next to the car, looking apprehensively at the gloomy clamminess. We had to head back home. And that meant the end of our journey. How about our own experiences? Briane had described it as such,

"Eye sees! Mouth shut! He makes hells and storms. He moves the four walls of universe. He terrifies young and old. Oh boy! That is Ogou Feray.

He fires a pot of klerin. He bathes everyone that goes by. He throws hot sauce in his eyes and seats unclothed over the pot. Oh boy! That is kouzin Zaka.

He comes down with Ayida. He Ramps and crawls everywhere. He breaks shells of crude eggs. He drinks them and eats cornstarch. Oh boy! That is Damballah.

Terrible! An arrow pierces her heart. She marries all the men. They all wear wedding band. Those who do not, she makes them impotent. Oh boy! That is Erzulie!"

On our way back home, we began to discuss what is next, we should be done in order to avoid the owl, Witner became so emotional to a point Briane had decided to change entirely her plan.

"I know for sure what needs to be done. Perhaps we should protect our home before anything else."

Briane was so impressed. Me, I headed back to my monastery just to find myself kneeling to pray the rosary upon my arrival.

Two days later, as much as I could remember, it is pouring all over the area. I woke up abruptly. Something had distressed me deeply over the night, but could it be a nightmare or a simple dream? Not at all. It was then that my telephone rang three times. At this ungodly hour I picked it up to see who dared to make such a call. I realized, it was not bad at all, it was Briane.

"I am so sorry. I probably disturbed your sleep at this early hour in the morning. I am sure you will not hold it against me. You know we had an unfinished business."

"Not at all, my dear. You did not disturb me. You know your voice means much to me. It is like the catalyst that stimulates my pulse. In fact, I was planning to meet you on my way back to school. Will 12 noon be better or 1 PM?" She said, "Any time you choose. I'll be okay with it." "That's fine to me Briane." I will just hit the shower's door.

At this point, Helena and Briane chose exactly 12 noon to invite me to their rendezvous. That is the time spirits would come down to the poto-mitan to meet with worshipers. But I noted I was not the only guest at the time. There was another guest of honor that Helena had met at the supermarket the week ago who turned out to be Dolores. So, she came upon Briane's approval to conduct a voodoo ritual for the family.

I was a bit angry and hungry too about that because I was kept in the dark. But I let it go, except to ask for one question.

"How did you get to convince her to do all of that for you, Briane?"

"That was Helena who initiated the contact in the open market one week ago. I desperately needed someone like her to help me. As you know Kootan, I cannot afford to lose everyone else remaining in the family following my mom's passage."

Dolores opened the ritual by asking everyone precisely present, the family member, to state the reason she was invited in that place. And I just discovered that day Briane had a secret shrine in a special corner of the house strictly reserved for Kitibel's loas.

The mambo went to that place. She blessed the artifacts as I called them. She sprayed fragrances over the attendees and all over the house. But when she reached me, she skipped me by fear of reprisal. Then, she pulled a huge Cuban cigar, set it up on fire. She exhaled smoke like chimney until Briane became in trance. I wondered if she was not possessed for the first time that day. And the lady quickly dismissed the loas who were present enormously. Now that was the time for the divertissement in that honor. And all I could say clandestinely, "My stomach has been chatting."

That day Helena served green plantain, water cress, avocado, boiled egg, and liver for breakfast at the dorm. I ate gigantically. I knew I would not be back too soon. My proposition was if I had to see Briane, I ought to skip the diner's time. After my morning session at school, I then decided to go and see Briane. But as soon as I got there, my wristwatch marked 12 o'clock noon. At this hour, every respectful in Port-Au-Prince, I knew the diner should be on the table. Helena shouted, "Please brother join us at the table. This is the diner's time." I said, "Yes, thanks sis!"

I agreed to participate in their banquet. I savored the most of the carbohydrate portion, du riz djon-djon (colorful rice mixed with mushroom), lambi (counch), yam, touffe beregene (match eggplant), avocado with pigmentate (spicy avocado) completed by some atomic jus (tropical fruit juice mainly made with papaya, orange, beet, mango, carrot with a final touch of carnation milk). That was not too bad at all. I said to myself, "Never mind the dorm dinner where I resided.

I think I get a better deal over here." I did not want to show my indifference so much to avoid being ridiculed. I bawled kind of ecstatically,

"Kitibel ain't even around to teach you anymore Helena. You still remained a superb cordon bleu (Chef)." She was thrilled and tearful for the remark. I thought they did not like me to enunciate Kitibel in this context. I groaned instantly.

"That was my fault people. I really had a bad day. I apologize for my statement." Briane jumped from her seat.

"No Kootan! We all know you. You were forgiven even before you have pronounced these words. Besides, you are categorically coming from Kitibel's wound; how could we think otherwise…you'd not ever talk disdainfully against none of us."

I felt so released to a point I exclaimed, "Enough Briane! We need to talk." I gathered everyone to a corner for a tete a tete.

"This time and once and for all, you should forget for the moment this owl's business. It seems to change your way of life even your characters. It has even affected me too. You need to concentrate instead in our education, sports, socialization, and else. Since our mother's death, we never enjoyed our lives. Movie theater, a good restaurant, discotheque for instances. We have the money. What can preclude us from enjoying life? Let us switch gear even for a while. Mother nature will take its course."

Everyone but me, growled in unison, "The time has really come, Briane."

Chapter III

Bankruptcy

Things got bad when Briane implemented several ethics to follow to survive. I witnessed that day when she established these principles. First, she wanted education to be a priority in the house. Second, it was acceptable to socialize with peers and go out on the weekend. Third, "They ought to be courteous and respectful as they were taught by Bonenfant." This time I alleged, "I also heard this one before as a Boy Scout." This impelled Briane to shout, "Thank you my love." Subsequently, to put aside the owl's concept, "We are not Kitibel. I don't believe we should be afraid of anything." She concluded, "Either it's a coward or waiting to strike again. The point is, we are not going to let this son of a gun disrupts our way of life. Mother nature will take its course."

Briane's good intention and Helena's willpower were not so pure. Helena was accustomed to do grocery on Saturday mornings. That was the day she hoped to get a ride to reach the Marche Fer so far distant. That day, it was different. She got out at an ungodly hour. She dressed like a princess. She sprayed herself with the best fragrances she could get her hand on. She hopped on one of the top-tap and took off suspiciously. What happened to Helena was hoping to find a gentleman to socialize. "At twenty-two years old if I keep going places with these kids, I will neither get a boyfriend nor get a family on my own," thought Helena. As soon as she got to the open market, the first person she met was a gentleman named Alanfer.

This man was known to be one of the wealthiest men among all the Bocor in Kenskoff's town located in the East of Port-Au-Prince. Even though he was a man barely in his fifties, his appearance and demeanor made him look in his twenties.

"Hey baby!" said Alanfer. Helena unexpectedly was not ready for it but assumed. She responsibly groaned, "Good morning Sir!"

"My name is Alanfer. I am an herbalist. You know… I am looking for herbs to prepare bathe for my client. I've been walking for at least half an hour, but I cannot find anything really appealing. I must attest surely, I do not know why when I pass by you the fragrance that you use seems to smell exactly what I want. So, mademoiselle (miss) would you please help me find the such fragrance?"

"Yes mister," said Helena, "I certainly will."

They walked side by side all over the place trying to find this exceptional aroma that continued to blow out mister

Alanfer's nose and had been nowhere to be found. Half an hour of search went by, nothing. They finally decided to take a pause. For Helena, it was a mission accomplished. As she dismissed Alanfer, the later realized this fragrance had begun to dismiss his nasal so sensual and sensible. And in about twenty feet apart from Helena this smell was completely gone. He yelled, "Hey mademoiselle, come back please. May I confirm if you have yourself the fragrance I wanted? Please do not leave me, you and I can certainly make a great couple if you accept me to be the love of your dream. You have been bombarding all over the scent, clearly the perfume I wanted. Would you mind going home with me baby please? And may I ask for your name?"

"Really, my name is Helena. I am working as a servant. I have been doing it since the age of seven. I don't believe you would ever accept a domestic for a partner of your life."

"But how do you know my love? How can you tell what makes the wind blow, the rain pours, somebody's internal desire as much as my feelings for you?" Helena seemed to be a little bit confused, "Sorry! I think you have a point."

"I would certainly like to hear a bit about yourself. Who you really are cherie…" Alanfer entered in his car and opened a bit ajar his driver's door hoping Helena would get in."? She did not. Instead, she advanced,

"As I said before, my name is Helena. Majority call me Nana. I was raised by a lady named Kitibel whom I called Aunty. Now she died. She was rich. She left a beautiful mansion, a lot of cash for her four children. Even though many including a huge dog called Cezin donated by a boy named Kootan had worked like slaves to produce all the wealth, she did not leave anything for us. Again, she left all for her four children who end up wasting everything for no reason. This is life." Alanfer inquired, "What was her name again?" "Kitibel," griped Helena.

"Oh! Kitibel," groused with emotion Alanfer. "Young lady, when the right time comes up, I will tell you a secret which you are not supposed to share with anyone. And you promise?" "I promise," responded the young girl.

"Now let me see if you know the great principle that Bocors use when people trivialize their secret."

"I believe it is a death sentence. 'Eye sees. Mouth remains close'."

"Ah Helena!" said Alanfer, "You really know your lesson. I say no more."

Helena replied yes to Alanfer! She promised to come back next weekend, at the same time. "Maybe you will share that secret with me, Pa." Helena said.

"Am I so old for you to call me Pa?" Alanfer said.

"Not at all! I was raised to treat people with respect. I will react differently next time I see you. Now I must return home to fulfill my duties. So long Sir!" responded Helena.

"So long Helena. I am confident that won't be for too long." Alanfer disappeared.

Now Helena returned home just to find Briane with a strange demeanor. "Hallo," said Helena. She added, "Don't give me this brashness Briane. You know I will not like it. By the way, I did not want to disturb your sleep. Both you and Witner studied so hard this week. I witnessed that. I know you are preparing for tests which I expect you to pass with good grades. I just took a top-top this morning. And from now on, I will probably do the same thing repeatedly. Don't take it wrong, won't you?" "Certainly not Helena," said Briane.

After all, Helena took care of the family better than ever before. The ritual meal that she constantly prepared on Sundays would be seen at the dining table in a daily basis since that time. Even Jack was inquiring, "God! What is going on with Helena? Her life seems to change suddenly. She does not dress sloppy anymore. She visits beauty salon more often. Her appetite changes, she even gained some weight." Enial teased her a bit hoping for a happy face, "What happened to you baby?" "Maybe she made a discovery such as her first boyfriend," suggested Jack. Helena yelled, "Don't even go there! You! Bunch of Misérables!"

Helena could not wait to see the following Saturday which seemed to recur so suddenly. She repeated the same trajectory from the last time. When she got there, Alanfer had already been waiting impatiently for her. As soon as he pulled a cigarette to calm down his emotion, Helena showed up. "Hi baby, I was beginning to lose faith. I thought you would not ever come," moaned Alanfer.

"Instead use this as an important lesson. Helena is always punctual, reliable, and very honest. I will never fail on those, you got it?" "Got you," said Alanfer.

Alanfer had been prepared for this visit. Since the beginning of the week preceding this visit, a luxurious hotel room and a reservation at a great restaurant had been paid for. All he expected from Helena is just to say, "Yes! I will go along with these arrangements." Luckily enough, Alanfer got everything he wanted.

That day, Helena claimed that she traced back since the day she was born, and she could not find anything that she could compare to the joy that she felt on that day.

"On my first date, all my passion just comes true in a click of a second. Really, how sweet are you LOVE."

Helena kept saying these words repeatedly until she got back home. But the worse of all, she decided to sacrifice everything for this love. She trusted Alanfer to a point where she gave her address to him and agreed to take off with him on the following Monday. Of course, this has been the day when the kids are in school. She would have the time to pack up and cook for the family before she departs. Sadly, she left the house under this heartbroken circumstance.

Now it was noon time, Briane would come back from school including Jack, Enial, and Witner that Monday. The dinner had been ready as usual, even a more complete dinner this time because a pot of atomic (fruit mixture with carnation milk) was served for appetizer.

"Helena! Helena! Helena, where are you?" said Briane. She repeated the call many times and she was nowhere to be found. She went to the back door, by the side, and the front door yelling Helena's name, she was not there. As she screamed Helena louder by the entrance's door, the noisy lady named Ametiz who resided next to her spotted Helena when she took off with Alanfer. "Hey baby! Do not waste your saliva anymore. I saw everything. This girl seems to be in love. I saw her living the house with an older man barely in his fifty today. It could have been 10am. Now you know." "Oh yes," groused Briane. Sadly, she said, "Thanks." She dismissed Ametiz with tears in her eyes.

When the boys heard the news, they too could not stop crying like déjà vu. It could not be any different when they lost their mother. Under these circumstances, Enial bellowed, "I told you, I knew she was in love." As for Jack, he screeched, "Helena is probably making out right now with this old man. Shut your mouth everyone, we will survive." Witner elected to come to the dinner table to enjoy the great meal, "I am so hungry. At least she prepared my favorite meal before she departed."

As per Briane's position, being the oldest, she was given the green light to be the primary caretaker of the family before Kitibel died. She felt it was a tough liability to assume in her situation. She ought to learn to live with it. She said, "Maybe my Mom probably had a determination in mind." She continued, "I will never regret this accountability because who else besides me. My Mom predicted right at the time. Yes! Helena disappeared and I don't even know where she stays at."

What one could not take away from Kitibel, as bad as she could be, is she raised these kids with a strict discipline. Whether she gave birth or not to them, she always maintained, "Value is important. I learned that from my Gran Mom. I must transmit that to you." Consequently, Helena, Debora, and Briane had a curfew, and even the boys, but, different in some respects.

No girls can get home late unless they are accompanied by one of the boys. As far as the males, they could not leave the house without the schoolwork been ready. And everyone in town knew it too. They gave Kitibel respect in this aspect. For her private life as an adult, only God knew. Consequently, this value ingrained so much in Helena, even after Kitibel's death she did not want anybody to know if she had moved with that man in her current situation. But rumors said otherwise. And I thought so too.

Helena took that decision because of Briane's attitude. I always warned her as a trusted friend. She would not listen to me this time. I saw her as another daughter Kitibel did not have, and a sister well deserved to Briane. She did not let her, for instance, have a say in the family's decision. Money was being spent for no reason. Helena like me thought that was a recipe for a disaster, "How far can our savings last if we don't restrain ourselves? Not even one of us can find a job," she thought.

She even grounded Briane. She did not want to wash her clothes anymore. When she prepared the meal, she expected her to do the dishes. Even though they hired an extra maid, she yet wanted Briane to get involved in physical work. "Aunty Kitibel died, and it is true. But that does not give you the freedom to waste every penny she had worked for," thought

Helena. But Briane ignored her advice. She agreed to buy each boy a brand-new car while they could have taken public transportation to go to school. Every weekend they went clubbing while their education is down the tube.

The boys for the first time liberated tremendously, even Briane. So as unhappy as she was, she saw the light of day. When I paid visit to their house, I found the boys making out with their partners. Helena shouted, "Oh Lord! What have you done? What has become to this family? That was not the way we were raised people," she could not think of being part of this miasma. That was the main reason for her disappearance.

Now Briane courageously continued to manage what her mom had left behind. Unfortunately, since Kitibel had not prepared a will, Briane did not know for sure what was left. Since then, she had been too busy to find time for herself. I found out about it later when I tried to advise her on management with the little, I knew on the subject. She told me repeatedly that she had rarely gone out on a date, and if she had agreed to go to the movies with an interesting fellow, she would bring Witner along—just to be safe.

Briane had attended a co-ed school where the little rich kids frequented. A handsome boy named Kemal had felt deeply in love with her. I thought Briane too did not hesitate a heck to promise her love back. She probably loved me too, but I hesitated too much to declare my intention to her. "This is what joining boy scout program had done to me," I thought. But up to this point all remained so secretive. She did not know how I was going to react. But I said to myself, "Who am I to say anything to her? Did I ever ask her out during those so many years of friendship?" Briane had decided to put her pride on the side and confront me.

In a routine visit to her house, she surprised me with these which I would never forget, "Kootan, I am in love with a boy named Kemal in my school, but do not worry about it, nothing will happen. I just believed the time has come for me to reach to this stage. So, I did. Kootan! You are not my boyfriend, I know. But I feel guilty and obligated to tell you this. And please forgive me if I hurt you."

That day, I was numbed, speechless. But I had the courage to show strength and consideration for her great honesty. I responded, "Briane! You already read my mind. The only thing I can say is, let mother nature take its course."

Briane guaranteed me that she had Witner to take her company if she ever had to go on a date with Kemal. Maybe to make her feel happy, I just groaned, "Don't feel so bad Briane. I will always be there for you, no matter what."

Of course, Witner would inquire about anything that comes to his mind. But I assured her that it was a good idea even though Witner's presence would frustrate her date. This boy would not keep his mouth shut. He was very protective of her and let everyone know that too. He was short, but he would wear boots—perfect for kicking hard. Perhaps he was acting out with the little I knew about this subject fear. It was the inevitable fear in his eyes that were cruel and unchecked by reality. He had his load too, nonetheless.

When Briane was out of town for a few days in a school trip, Enial and Jack would take charge and bully Witner all day long. Briane could rarely sleep well at night. It was not insomnia either. What was becoming of her? It was not clear to me at all. Was she unhappy? Was she traumatized about the owl or loss of her mom, even Helena's disappearance? Yes, she was. The reality was she is too secretive. No one was able to penetrate the hard shell she covered herself with. She adhered to the unwritten code of womanhood as strictly as she knew how because her family value should be protected. She would not consider anything that would make her heart pound absurdly.

Briane had bleached her hair, lost strands of it from a cheap perm, and wore a bandana to cover it. She sewed and beginning to look just like her mother. Her beauty and mannerisms made her quite exotic. Men would offer her a ride when she used to pick up Helena from the open market. The hell with them, she would say. She would not mind hopping on a *Tap Tap* (a minivan). In fact, she would go as far as to pay an extra fee to sit in the front with Briane to avoid the charlatans in the back. They had bothered her many times before and made advances and reciting lines she did not think were humorous or clever. But the Tap Top's driver almost rear-ended an ambulance. She screamed her lungs out before he slammed on the brake.

It had been such a vivid memory. She would make no fuss about it now. In retrospect, she was pleased to have saved her life and those of the passengers.

The secret of her life thus carried a false speculation, and it was entirely her fault. She could not be persuaded to do things she did not know about. Lately, she would have to be in a convulsed aberration if she were to talk about her emotion. It was a pleasure to listen to her rave about the mistreatment of children in public schools even though she never spent a day in that system. She spoke about her lack of confidence in the whole process. It was even amusing to hear her talk about being a rebel hoping ideas would change things without action.

She was sweet too. I had admired her for that. Yet she bore a deep grudge for me. I could never understand why. Sometimes she would mock or tease me, though she dared not go too far. There were days she would prefer not to think about her responsibility and routine or to talk about her love and desires. But that was one of those rare days when she was very personable.

In the backyard, she showed me the plants. Almost immediately, my mood lifted. I wished I could hold her hands.

"You used to talk about your days as a Boy Scout."

"Yeah, I remember those days." I responded.

"Why did you leave home when you were so young?" She asked while buttoning her white blouse up to her neck.

"I was unhappy. I was clinically depressed." I began to stutter. The words could hardly come out of my mouth. I could not take my eyes off her. I was on pins and needles but was hardly terrified. I could not think straight.

Briane said, "Are you okay Kootan? Tell me what infuriate you? Lately, I read you as a different person."

I knew it was just the acceptance of Kemal that irritated me but, I fake it instead, "My education Briane. I neglected that part of my life significantly."

"Everything will be fine." Briane said and dismissed me.

Just in time to sign up for my classes. As a rule, I had to study Physics and Math. I took a top-top to the University. I paid my tuition fee, so I was a happy camper. Thoughts spinning, I jumped over the school fence and landed on the said street. I did my best to make sure I was not being followed. Next thing I saw, Briane. I was being followed. She wanted to make sure I was doing the right thing. She ordered me to get in her car and she drove me to her house.

"What are you running from?" asked Briane.

I was both surprised and happy to see her. I approached her with a smirk she was by now accustomed to.

"First, I'm heading home. Then I'm going to buy me some books."

"You'll do just fine."

"So, will you. This is your last year, right?" I blurted out.

"Yeah but I expect it to be hard. There's a lot going on in my life." She said and waited.

"So, I heard."

It came to my surprise that she asked about Cezin's condition. I knew I was right on the money. Breathless, I explained that I saved the dog's life and what it would cost to keep me alive. She offered to pitch in. I said, "It is not about the money. It is the time-consuming responsibility I put the father in. I don't even know if he is really happy or not." But though my cash flow was running low, I declined.

"Gee, Turenne would have been happy to have Cezin." She said, as if she were right.

Enial said, "There was a time when he wanted the dog, but I haven't heard about him for months." I responded, "Anyway I think the dog is in good hands, even in better hands than you, where no owl wont dare reaches him."

Everyone thought that was funny, launched at that. Subsequently, Briane pulled me on the side all the way to the balcony to discuss some of her private matters.

"I'm worried about Enial. He quits school, he does not study, and he plays soccer with peers about ten hours a day. He's driving us all crazy." She said calmly. I knew exactly what she meant. What she did not say was that she was in debt because her brothers wanted to be with the johns.

That is what Helena has anticipated. She bought cars, but they could not afford gas and maintenances. She kept supporting them, though her finances were draining.

"Ask Father Bonenfant to talk to them," as per my proposition.

"They listen to no one. Well, Kootan, I must go now. I hope to see you again soon. What's your plan for Saturday night?"

"No plan so far. Why?"

"We are going to a party. Don't you want to join us? You know Kemal is a Christian. He only goes to Church." She quipped.

"Sure. I would love to. Where?" I was excited.

"Cabane Choucoune. Come get us at seven, will you?" Sure said.

That place was the most popular nightclub in town. Not because it was located on the beach nor its size, but it is the crowd. Everyone, Jack, Witner, and Enial summoned their partners to report to that nightclub. Of course, it is going to be a fabulous night. Money was being spent regardless. Like a downpour rain, alcohol gulped down all night long, nonetheless.

Cabanne Choucoune consisted mostly with army officers in uniform, drug dealers and scam artists who liked to flaunt cash, and of course, guys like us. I thought about my forthcoming date with Briane as the days went by. I would be punctual. As a matter of fact, I was. We got there on time. But, as usual, there was a long line. Since we both dressed appropriately, we could get in very quickly, of course, not for nothing. Some fat tip!

My favorite band, Bossa Combo, was about to perform. Meanwhile, the famous actor and comedian Languichatt had already occupied the podium. He brought some energy, a lot of it. He was so inspirational.

Now there you go my two favorite bands, so spectacular, "Taboo Combo and Skasha." I had a great time. It was an exceptional and unforgettable moment.

Briane was not too engaging. If she had tried to conceal her awkwardness, she failed to do so. I sensed what the heck was going on. She was mad at her friend, Kemal, whom she had not heard for more than a month. The man she liked to brag about. Surely, he was full of integrity and ambition. A religious fanatic too! He said he was going to be a medical doctor and a minister. But, as I told her, he was a mere show-off.

We were dancing. I felt her breasts against my chest, her nipples tingling. I rested my hands on her waist. More than that, I caressed her strong-boned face.

"Tell me what's going on, Briane?" I asked politely.

"Not only that my finance is not so good, but also, I'm going to break up with Kemal." She said.

"That would be a good choice if you ask me. You can do better, much better." I affirmed. She asked me to take her back home. Elbowing our way through the crowd, we exited the club.

Two days later, Briane summoned me to her house. Excitement overcame me. When I arrived, I found her writhing in agony. She looked terrible. She did not want to eat nor drink. She was losing weight fast.

"Let's take her to the emergency room." I said to Enial.

"Good idea, Kootan. I hate to see her suffer," said Jack, out of concern.

Enial drove her to the hospital where she was given drugs and fed intravenously. In less than three hours, she was released.

The next day, I visited her, and, to my great surprise, I stumbled into her making out with Kemal on the patio. I excused myself.

"Don't be silly." My presence seemed to bother Kemal. Why was he so "Thank you," I said as I sat down?

I spilled juice all over my neck and shirt. I hated to see Briane so miserable. I was thinking about her and me together as one. It was not happening. Under these circumstances, I would never be told what kind of mistakes I made. I wanted to find out why she had chosen him over me. I came to realize that feeling came and went, and love was more than just a word. As the saying goes, "Love is like a river. You drink it, but it won't quench your thirst." How ungrateful and disrespectful she was towards me, I wondered aloud. Claimed that my generosity was obviously a problem, which prompted Kemal to hop on his car and speed away.

Nevertheless, that night was incredibly special to mr. I received messages from somewhere and felt obligated to splurge them everywhere. I just smelt danger as the late Helena, but without being able to stop it. Then I ventured to offer this advice,

"Briane you need to cut down on your expenses. No party on weekends. You might need to consider entertaining students here. The rooms are huge, and the bathrooms are decent. Rent some rooms to girls. If you take my advice, things might improve."

Unfortunately, I was not taken seriously. The boys did not follow my advice. The servants fought against being laid off. At the end, they lost their house.

There was a hurricane. Merchants, bus drivers, students, teachers, and animals hid to a safe place. The worst was yet to come.

Lightning struck their home. Half of the enclosure was gone, one fifth of the roof caved in. I rescued them.

Then when it was over, all emotion passed. Now the house needed extensive repairs. The national bank approved a loan for repair. It took three exceptionally long months to put the place in shape.

Meanwhile, Briane, including the brothers, had moved to Kemal's home temporarily, pending the outcome.

At nineteen years old, Briane lost hope and confidence, and she even desired to come back to Valparaizo to regain strength.

One afternoon, a messenger showed at my front door.

"Briane wants to see you."

"Could it be anything tragic in the family? I said to myself. "What would she need me for?" *I remained in the dark.*

"I'd be there in a minute if not sooner. Is anybody sick? Is there any trouble there?" I gasped for an answer.

"No sir," said the messenger.

I did not have a car, not even a bicycle. I called for a taxi and managed to get there as soon as possible. When I got to the house, Kemal's residence, I was told that one of Briane's brothers was engaged in a fight with Kemal. The other two, Jack and Enial took side with their younger brother. She did not know what to do. She was looking for a solution.

Kemal's choice was either to swallow his anger or get rid of everyone. His family was zealous, devoted, and religious. They would not tolerate nonsense. I found a solution, which happened to be the best for them.

We all gathered and said this prayer that Father Bonenfant taught me to say in adversity. Together we cited psalms 23 and 91. Then I asked the boys to move in with me, until their home was completed. They accepted the offer, and I was glad they did.

"Kootan, you're really our savior, Kitibel and Pepe who are no more with us. And thank you on behalf of this family Big Bro!" alleged Witner.

Briane took the day off from everyone. She went to visit Dolores to put up some mazonzon for her. She anticipated to find an allez mieux (the situation would be better) through that channel, but things did not get to go too well when she was caught in the house evocating the loas. Fortunately, Pastor Zenas was never informed about it.

This time I knew it was my turn to join in this situation. Although Briane had done so many stupid things which could disrupt our relationship, but what about the things of values we had cherished for so many years since our childhood? Nope! I would not leave her ever for just her mistakes. I would have been then the stupid one. Besides, her mom would have been so disturbed in grave if I ignored their call when I am needed the most.

Three months later, before they could settle in, when they got home after schooling, they got a note from the bank stating that if they failed to make accumulated payment amounting twenty thousand dollars on their house it would go on foreclosure. Briane had never been to this stage on her lifetime so short before. She did not even know what foreclosure was. Not even one payment was made.

To make the matter worse, their life savings was gone. The boys fought and engaged in brawl daily. The bank account, in which their beloved mother had deposited a large sum of money over time, was now reduced to nothing. How much money they spent was less relevant than what they now owed.

Some speculated that it had been more than a quarter of a million dollars. I could not understand for the life of me how Kitibel could have possibly left that kind of sum. A sum, I had once a bet against. If Briane, of all people, had no clue, all guesses were wrong.

I was summoned to go see Briane because Enial was terribly sick. This time I became annoyed because I was studying for an exam. I wondered what the best way was to handle that situation. I was not a doctor. They knew that. Enial had been out the night before, partying. They knew that too. Briane was concerned. All Briane was talking about to go and see Dolores, Alanfer, Docima, and even Alcika who had been dead way back. She seemed very confused. She thought the owl had returned. The pact ought to be settled.

So, I did what she should have done a few hours earlier: I drove Enial with having his family to his side to the local medical center where he was diagnosed with mild fever. Suddenly Jack pulled Briane to his side, "Remember how Debora started with when she died? Can it be that history is repeating itself?" She responded, "You dare not coming back with this owl's affair. I am trying not to remember this tragic past in our life. Why don't you look for a treatment for your brother?"

"Enough Briane," said Jack and moved aside.

Upon my return, they told me about Enial's condition over dinner. They expressed shock and concern but settled on the fact that he was alive. What I concealed from them was that I had just dropped Enial over his former girlfriend's home. Witner and Jack, who were trying to blame it on Kemal for having been of no help, thanked me a few times. I noticed Briane blushing.

"You always come up with a solution, Kootan. You're a genius." Witner said.

I responded, "I am not a genius. I just think fast."

"I want you to know that you will always be welcome in this house."

Kemal did not seem to like what he was hearing. In fact, he hated it. My friendship to his girlfriend was a major concern to him.

"Guys take these two tickets. Go see a show tonight." Kemal said, handing them to Witner, who furiously declined. I said not a word, but I was in cohorts with Witner.

"Briane, would you agree that Kootan is smarter than . . .?"

Witner was saying when she interrupted.

"Stop it. You sound childish." She said, while cleaning the table.

"I think I'm the stranger here. Have fun, everybody. I'm out." Kemal said.

She felt the need to reprimand Witner.

"I need to talk to you, Kemal." He said, "I'll be waiting outside," and slammed the door behind him.

Chapter IV

The Children in Shambles

Briane was mad—mad as she did in most cases since she got into relationship with Kemal. She spattered beside me and got down to business. She showed me a letter from the National Bank. The letter was explicit. No fine print! The bank, which was under, starts the foreclosure proceeding in about a month if Briane makes no significant payment. "I can sell my car," Witner said, trying to appease her. "Oh Witner! That was exceedingly kind of you. How about you Jack and Enial? Are you not worried sick as well in front of this situation? Why didn't you make the same offer?"

Jack could not care less. Enial responded, "I already lost my mother. This car now represents my greatest asset. How can you expect me to dispose it this way? Let the house go to foreclosure!

Witner snapped emotionally, "Briane! My car has been ready to go. You can sell it any time you wish."

"Thanks once again brother. But your car does not worth much. Besides, that might not even cover a mortgage." She retorted. Witner suggested that they should sell all the cars to come up with the money owed. It was over thirty thousand dollars. Why had she failed to pay the bills? Easy, she had no paying job. I made her realize she would need to set aside the legal fee. Soon thereafter, she sold the cars for a whole lot less. What would she do now since she fell short? One thing I reminded her was that the bank was serious in its request and was leaning towards the foreclosure more than anything else. Briane listened to me, tried to borrow money from some friends to no avail, and sold her jewelry.

Three weeks later, the house was put in auction for sale. But even though the mortgagor could do something, they only raised nine thousand. They owned more money than that. It was just enough to rent an apartment. Now how would they take care of their basic needs such as food, clothing, and public transportation?

It was indicated to her that if she could meet the deadline, the house was going to be put up in the market for sale. She had managed to rent a small apartment I had found for her on my own. Yet, the boys could not care less. That had not been easy. In fact, I had showed her a few, just to make up her mind. Not one had been good enough. Either the kitchen had been too small, or the bathroom would need a major repair. I had become exhausted at this point. I had once told them that their situation was critical, so much so they could not be so choosy.

"Such is life," I said to her.

"Who would have thought we would be enduring such a hard time?" She wondered aloud.

"Anyone can lose his or her fortune. I have seen and heard it happen too many times." I added, to encourage her.

"Tell us about it," Enial said as he stood there. "This is not a joke."

There was a strange grin on Briane's face, and her hand was extended imploringly toward me. Taken by surprise, I offered her some comfort and truly meant that too. She asked me to take her to the new landlord so she could finalize the transaction and got the keys to her new place.

"You saved us, my friend," she said, as soon as I agreed.

"I'll do anything for you, my love. You know that." I said, in a flattering tone.

"I know. I'm grateful for that." She replied quickly.

"Someday I might need you to do something for me." I uttered.

"Like what? Wash your dirty underwear." She said, jokingly. Everything happened in place. Briane was a tad less crazy and worrisome. I felt a sense of accomplishment—something they themselves acknowledged. I was about to lock the door behind me when I saw the mailman drop a letter in my mailbox. I wondered what it contained, good news I hoped.

"This is to inform you that Cezin had died. It happened suddenly after a long week of sickness. I personally took him to the clinic. I was told he had a virus. He was given a shot, but it did not work. I did the best that I could, but his condition went from bad to worse. Unfortunately, he is gone. I buried him near his old shed where he laid bare in his final hours. Please, inform Kitibel's kids of his passing. And I do not think it had to do with the owl. I hope these words bring you peace and comfort at this time of sorrows. Peace! Father Bonenfant."

"Oh my God, Cezin died." I yelled to the top of my lung. THE QUESTION REMAINED. SHOULD I CONVEY THE MESSAGE TO THESE KIDS? Finally, I did. But what would Enial say or do? How about Witner who had once threatened to break my windows because the dog was still far away? When I told them about it, moments later, they all expressed shock. Briane shed tears and Witner banged his head against the wall.

Enial remained calm as he was repeating a famous Biblical verse. Jacques was just listening. "Such is life. Here today, gone tomorrow." Enial said. "How old was Cezin?" Witner inquired. "I don't quite remember." I answered, trying to not think hard.

"I bet you Fransic would kill him and eat him too." Witner said. "No, he didn't in the past." I was saying before being interrupted. "Ah-ha-ha, I can't believe you're defending Fransic for what you went through with this bastard." Briane said. They all laughed and pointed fingers at me. The laughter was dissolved into stillness.

Briane asked me to join her in the kitchen. I was no longer in the mood to reminisce about Cezin's past life, and certainly not to talk about school. I hesitated.

"What can I help you with?" "What's the rush? Got somewhere to go?" "As a matter of fact, I do. The woman in my study group is coming over. She needs help in math and physics. And so, I volunteered." I said, knowing full well it was a lie.

"That's your girlfriend?" She sounded astonished. "Come on, you can tell me. I promise I won't tell anybody."

Briane would not tell anyone? Now that was funny, hilarious even. "I won't date until you get married." I stammered.

"Then, let us just agree, you'll never date. All right." She replied, with cynicism all over. Was she about to drop a bombshell? How stupid I was she had already done so. Evidently, she and Kemal were planning to break up after two long and arduous years. She might have been jealous over a girl, but that was not it. There was no good reason but a perfect excuse, Kemal was an ardent religious fanatic and she was not.

There was more to it. It is dated back three months before, as an active member in the Catholic Church and often quarreled with Kemal's father over the meaning and interpretation of biblical verses. The feud among them now seemed to cause uproar in Briane's relationship. "How could his father dare to have said Briane was not the right girl for his son?" I said to myself.

"To Kemal's father, if you are catholic, you're a perpetual sinner. You will not be forgiven. Therefore, you're going straight to hell."

He had said it many times. Whether or not he had himself believed that was impossible to tell. He had surely irritated her over time. And grief had been followed. So, Kemal audaciously told her that he thought he should follow his own parents' advice by ending the relationship. Nonetheless since he loved her, he was going to continue with her. No doubt, she was furious. Feeling insulted too. "That's what he says. But there must be another motive."

"At the very least, Kemal seems to be honest. He doesn't want to waste my time." "Besides, love is like a twin river. They float left and right. One may take you to the shore and the other may lead to the ocean. If it were your choice, you'd choose the first."

"There is an answer for everything. The important thing is, choose something to believe in. No one is supposed to force you to have faith in something you don't feel comfortable with." I implore to Briane.

Meanwhile while Briane thought about the loas to solve her problems, I never ceased to pray for her soul. Morning, noon, and evening time following Bonenfant's advice to avoid the worse, "Satan seems to be real, with only two psalms hoping that her family will find peace."

Kemal intervened under this circumstance pretending to expose his religious dogma on Briane, "Baby! You could make an extremely devoted Christian. How about becoming a born again one?"

"Oh no!" said Briane, "You are so Christian you did not even know if Christian had numerous denominations. I may not be a Baptist, but I am still a Christian." Kemal shouted,

"Enough Baby! I think you are right. You have just met me, and you never put the time to talk to me. You do not even know me so much. But only one thing, I am so pure as a Catholic and voodooist. I never let you put your hand under this skirt."

Kemal stood up furiously, "I know your true partner had been and will always be Kootan. Who else would dare to know you better than that one?"

Briane bounced back and forth like a ping pong ball feeling offended,

"Boy! Do not even try to go there. Kootan seems to be your problem. This is not about Christian and else. I can leave this place to join the homeless at Sun City right now," frightening like pussycat. Suddenly, Kemal genuflected.

"Briane, I beg you for forgiveness. I did not really mean to insult you by my statement. Will you?" She felt so frantic and tears restlessly poured down her face.

"I accept your apology. Maybe my emotion had occupied my inner self. We will straighten that out."

"So, how about a hug," Kemal said.

All arguments settled. The couple remained ever sweeter than before. But the day after, Briane summoned me to meet with her at her brothers' rental apartment, she needed me so badly. I ought to show up in hurry. I had found Briane in an ecstatic mood. But sometimes something that pleased someone might turn out to be bitter for another.

She lectured me about her grumble with Kemal, I was disappointed. I would rather see their relationship falling apart instead of reconciliation.

"I will never have my day with Briane despite all I endured for her." I thought. But as a former boy scout, I ought to cultivate COURAGE. I surely did. All turned out to be a simple joke to me.

Three days later, I received a letter from Isabel to come in person to see her. She lived so far, in Valparaizo. I have yet begrudged going back there if not for an important reason. I finally decided without thinking twice to hop the first public transportation to go and meet with her. Briane would get an explanation when I come back. But all along the road, I felt displeasure at the same time tremendous joy because I had not seen Isabel for quite a while, I missed her enormously.

It was displeasure. I expected to have a clue for the reason of my displacement. This incited me to guess so many things on my own, "My father already died in jail. Maybe Kiti herself is so sick, I wanted to become her private trustee before she dies. Or simply because she just wanted to see me. I may be missed." I thought.

When I got there, I greeted her so gently. She grabbed me like a precious treasure. She took me straight to the dining table and shouted, "You must be so hungry and angry after eight hours ride to get to Valparaizo. But do not worry. I have an explanation for all of that." I responded,

"How dare you to even think like that Isabel. Don't you know you are my Mom and no one else and I love you Sis."

Two torrents of tears were dripping from her eyes. She anticipated an insult, "Too much for me to tolerate. You know I am so emotional." She shouted, "Follow me."

She took me to the dining room. She inquired about Kitibel's kids, each one individually. But when she got to Briane, she wanted to know how she managed as the head of the family. I said, "With the grace of God and my input, everything goes smoothly so far."

Now she commanded me to have dinner with her, "It is quite a long time we did not get to eat together Kootan..." I responded, "Surely, you are right."

Now, I became very impatient. I wanted to get down to business, the reason she summoned me, "What is going on Isabel? Anybody dies? Or else, tell me the truth."

"Oh, there you go Kootan. As you know, you grew up with me. With my dad and your mom's permission, I raised you not as a brother but my own blood. You will suffer a lot should something happen to me. To make this short, I went to my doctor last week. I did a lot of tests and one of them revealed that I have cancer in my left breast. And I only have six months to live after the diagnostic."

"Oh Sister, I would condemn you forever if you did not make this move. And let me thank you for summoning me. This is really a cause for such alarm, and I thank you for it." But only one thing I would like to know is what I can do to give your life. Maybe I should quit school to come and live with you? I won't mind doing that."

"Not at all! Isabel insisted. Go back to the capital to resume with your schoolwork Kootan." Isabel said.

In this current situation I went back to the capital with great deal of emotion just to find myself into even deeper emotion. Briane announced to me that soon she would have to travel. She claimed that everything had been arranged by Kemal's father. He had been for a while praying to God to give me direction. He felt I looked too young to assume my responsibility. He said he had written the head of his congregation and made demand to grant me scholarship to go and study abroad. Again, his cry had been answered.

"Now, Kootan, I would have to leave these boys under your strict supervision. I hope you don't mind," said Briane.

"I surely will in this case."

"By the way," said Briane. "How was your trip to Valparaizo?" inquired Briane.

"Well, nothing to brag about. I went there just to come back with a broken heart." "Kiti informed me that she went to the doctor. She was told that she has cancer in her left breast."

Briane was astonished to learn this bad news, "Oh my second Mom Kiti, God help us. I don't want to lose her like my Mom."

"Unfortunately, she only has six months to live." Kootan paused. "The question I wonder is how am I going to survive with both economically and emotionally?" Briane lamented, "Don't say that baby. That will make it two human beings in consternation, you and me." Kootan yelled, "Oh not Briane, enjoy yourself to the full potentiality in life. This is my turn. You suffered enough, baby." Briane, responded, "It's not quite my fault, frankly. This agony resides deeply into my heart. We must suffer together."

"Briane, I feel that I did not waste any second spent with you throughout my short life. Now I understand what our friendship means."

Briane kind of tested me that day, "What does our friendship meant to you?"

"It is bigger than the moon, any spheres up there, the cosmos if you would." "The infinite too, since you want to be an engineer."

We just gazed at each other and said, "So long."

Three months later, we planned a peregrination to Valparaizo to visit my sister.

She was so happy to see us. We showered her with various types of flowers and gifts. We agreed before we left not to verse not even a single tear for her. She also was Briane's Godmother. She was told to come back for a second check up with some specialist from the United State of America. She would certainly let us know the findings. I said, "That would be awesome. We surely accomplished us objective, let us return to the capital."

One week later, Pastor Zenas, Kemal's father summoned Briane to come to his office. When she got there, she was handled a package and was demanded to travel immediately before September 1. Everything was planned since they received her documents far back in June. Now, if she failed to show up, she would run the risk to jeopardize her position at the University. Yes! All her documents were sent far back in June, she did not expect to be called so fast while scores of people had been waiting in line for the same reason.

Now an emergency meeting among the family was planned. Kemal of course had been invited to attend. This meeting was scheduled to take place at the boy's residence on Sunday. The time was fixed for one o'clock after service precisely to accommodate Kemal.

On my way to that meeting, I decided to drop by to one of Kitibel's friends to pick up a letter that she sent me. And since I was running out of time, I said to myself when I got there, I would be pluckier. Then I would proceed to open this letter.

Throughout the meeting, questions such as who would keep eyes on Witner as the youngest, who would be in charge of the choices, and settle disputes in the house, etc. under these circumstances, I fleetingly stood up and demanded if I might read a letter from Kiti. Everyone screamed in unison, "Surely you may. Besides, it is an honor Kootan." I opened the envelop, pulled the letter, and began to lecture,

"Hello Kootan, it is an honor to communicate with you today once again. I can stop thinking about your brief with Kitibel gang so far in Valparaizo. Give my regards to every single one of them. Now the main reason for this correspondence is to let you know that I was found cancer free. It was a huge mistake from their part to misdiagnose me so wrong. But what makes me so sad is not the mistake. I wonder how many others lost their lives for the same reason. Please, I feel fine presently and already begin to conduct my activities as usual. Thanks for your support and so long."

Everybody yelled, "God is great! I knew something was wrong." Briane stood up and said,

"What Isabel stated in this letter captures my attention enormously. I foresaw it since I was a kid. That reinforces my intention to pursue my goal to become a great medical doctor. I hope I will be able to help my people someday."

Now it seemed that this unexpected Isabel's announcement had put an end to that meeting. Everybody unexpectedly came out satisfied, which incited to vociferate, "How great are you Almighty God," on and on again. Three weeks later.

The day of departure had been set. It seemed another had been lost once again in this the family in both sides. Briane and her entire crowd. As for me I could not handle myself because it occurred to me as a shortfall, something unaccomplished, "Am I ever going to see this girl ever again? One says for many, once they go abroad, they forget about everyone they left behind." Anyhow, I thought, I ought to learn to live with it. Life goes on.

On the actual day of the farewell, the atmosphere had been very gloomy and so the people are sad. Kemal showed up ahead of the time by refusing to let her leave without testing the final look of her presence. Gosh, it was a forever hug and stare which made Witner screeched, "What about me Kemal? I need a chance to say goodbye to my sister." We all joke about it to a point to make Enial bawled, "Hay Kemal! Get in the luggage, you would be better off."

Suddenly the chauffeur arrived. Briane hugged everyone for the last time. To me, nothing but tears, she did not have the courage to even regard me. I shrieked, "BB! I understand. So long."

Briane taxied while the crowd intoned, "Ce n'est qu'un aurevoir mes freres…Ce n'est qu'un aurevoir…Comme Dieu nous l'a promis mes freres…Ce n'est qu'un aurevoir." Briane disappeared in the haze.

Chapter V

Briane Moves Abroad

Briane left Haiti to study abroad; but, back home, things had gotten worse in some respect. Anyhow, she wasted no time to accommodate herself with New York City's life. She wanted first to recoup what she had lost back home and tried to dismiss the idea that an owl was following her. "I will survive. I am Briane, not Kitibel. I should not pay for her mistakes," thought Briane.

Briane joined a club called, "Students alliance of City College." This new contact allowed her to master the college environment within and out including the five boroughs of New York City in a short time. As far as her curriculum, she was accepted as a freshman in a fast tract program called biomed program because she was the recipient of a scholarship for that program.

Meanwhile from Haiti, I dedicated myself to her brothers as she would her herself. And I missed her so much, as she appealed how much she suffered of my absence. She kind of aggravated the situation profoundly. The worse of it, in her communications, Briane had informed me just after two months of absence Kemal had already offered to break up with her. She claimed she was not upset at all about it because she already felt it was coming. All the diligences and courtesy toward her at her departure were nothing but fakes. But she believed Kemal should have gotten the gut to declare it face to face to her and not after already being overseas.

I wrote her immediately expressing my dissatisfaction for what he did in which I mainly stressed, "What are the charges for the separation after all? I hope it is not because of me?" She responded,

"Not for you Kootan. On the contrary, he always thought by having you so close to me, his interest would be protected. You would not let other guys approach me easily. But I honestly believe, Catholic faith versus Baptist had been the main reason for it." "Remember!" said Briane, "His father is a Baptist minister and so is he, while I am a devoted Catholic."

Now, then I realized I was protected. God had preserved her sanctity for me. The part I appreciated the most, she told me confidentially, she never let Kemal penetrated in her womanhood. He never tried either. She made it clear for him that could only happen after marriage. "Knowing young boys and girls today, this is something to appreciate."

I thought. And that was so encouraging. She prompted me to accomplish even faster the tasks she ordered me to execute.

I paid visit to her brothers almost every weekend or so to inform her of their progress. The last time I went to see them they were making progress in school. That was encouraging. Witner and Jack never failed to throw me all their rhetorical questions hoping to stick me. But knowing the kind of guy I was for what he did, they never succeeded. Enial was a little bit closer to me in age. He always showed maturity when we were together. Instead he would praise me as always for being there for them far back elementary school. That was also encouraging to me. Meanwhile I devoted my time in my education. I would not disappoint my family in respect for Isabel.

I was used to join a specific group every Saturday morning to practice math and physics. Afterward, I would proceed to Briane's clique to check on them. And, since I was used to buy them some grocery before I got there, I dropped by the Marche-fer to get them what I felt necessary. But guess who I saw wandering around? Helena.

She shouted, "Kootan! Kootan! Kootan! How are you?" I retorted ardently, "Helena! Where have you been?" We stared at each other endlessly until she bellowed.

"Kootan! I will explain everything, do not worry. But, I have so much to say, it will take hours to explain before I will let you go, if you don't mind." I said, "Surely, I would not mind."

"First of all, what brings you to this place and I am sure you would want to say the same about me?" I responded,

"I, too, have so many things to say, and without wasting no time, let's go down to business."

"Number one, these kids as predicted, had lost everything. The boys handed up living in a rental quarter while Briane was forced to move with Kemal's family."

"Number two Briane is presently living overseas studying medicine in New York City with the help of Kemal's father," I quipped, "About you, tell me something Helena."

She could not stop crying posing her head on my shoulder, and when the time had come, she shouted,

"No Kootan! This is rather hard that, but my alibi will be much worse than that."

"First of all, Aunty Kitibel is still alive. I see her everyday face to face. But there is nothing I can do about it." I became short of breath and about to be fainted. A bystander quickly handed me some fresh water. Helena advanced, "Are you okay Kootan? I am so sorry." "I am fine. And what is next Helena?" "When I left the house with the old man you were informed about that. I know Briane told you. Well!" she continued, "Yes! I admit I was in love but, my boyfriend convinced me to take off with him and he had a secret to tell me. It took me three months after he used me before he hallowed me to know his covert."

"Now this is it," said Helena, "As I was resting with him in a cool Saturday night, he popped up to my ears what I would not rather want to hear, 'Kitibel is living right here with us and many others,' I thought I was hallucinating. But do you know something Kootan? He took me to a special quarter where they keep zombies (people that still alive after being buried). The first person I saw was Kitibel in addition to five others." Helena continued, "But she did not recognize me. She kept her head down and not allow to lift it up."

"I strolled all over the place and demanded to get out from this relationship. And to make this matter short, he tried to calm me down by giving his own explanation.

"Helena, you cannot deny you did not know if I am a Bocor. You knew what I do for a living. I must confess I did not kill Kitibel personally. But I am in the market of buying and selling zombie. So, I bought Kitibel from an undisclosed name Bocor about one year ago. In fact, the seller was not the killer. He sold the lady to an undisclosed one using the voodoo's principle, "Ge we! Bouch pe!" whom in turn sold it to me." Alanfer said.

"Now she is for sale. I do not intent to keep her here. The price on her head is five thousand dollars due to her rank in the society in her lifetime. How can I be blamed for what others do?" Alanfer paused.

"If you ever denounce me or intent to disclose this to anybody, you already know what the penalty will be. Got it." Helena questioned him,

"Are you saying you are going to kill me if I happen to disclose this to somebody else?" He flattery responded, "No Helena! Not me! The forces will. Not me! You see!"

Helena detailed her relationship with Alanfer from start to present. She kept me for an additional two hours to brief me her situation, how much she would like to come back home to take care of Enial, Jack, and Witner, but she was scared to death to escape. She did not even know what is going to happen to her for disclosing this paraphernalia. But I gave her all the information she needed to know in case she escaped. And I guaranteed her that Briane would be incredibly happy to have her back. I walked her to the bus station. When I got there, I realized her bus was DIEU PANOU, a well-known vehicle by so many. She boarded immediately because she was so late. She was in a hurry. Alanfer was waiting for some merchandises whose mostly herbs and different fragrances. Then she disappeared in the fog.

Aftermath, I was afraid of the repercussion of this confidence with Helena, "Really was I supposed to know this top secret? Can Helena really suffer shock in return for deliberately disclosing this voodoo stuff?"

I kept my mouth shut. I dare not to discuss this thing with anyone, even with Briane because I must save my own life at all course. I just happened to realize once more that voodoo had been real. I might have to be incredibly careful when dealing with this stuff.

Surprisingly, the day after, on my way to these kids home, since I was unable to make it on Saturday, I dropped by a news stand to buy a newspaper. The first thing I read was the tragic accident that DIEU PANOU was wiped out while crossing one of the unbridged rivers. That vehicle submerged, not even a single body was recovered. But rumors reported that there was an owl flying around the bus before such accident happened. I said to myself, "There you go again. Welcome back on your return, mister owl."

What a surprise for these kids even Briane so far in New York State! And no one believed this quandary. But that was real, except, I dared not disclose the truth about what alleged Helena.

I was bombarded by questions with every one of them, even Briane in our correspondences. I answered as many as I could. My conscience had been so clear, my heart pure, and I was ready to go ahead with a load on my back without knowing when I would be delivered. But it was not all of it. The worse had yet to come.

My heart was broken down. When I summoned that Witner did not come home for many days. But since the day we had taken Briane to the airport he acted stubbornly. He thought he was too big to be supervised as Briane had wished. Witner had never behaved as such. So, our concern grew exponentially. He had never committed any delinquent act, so we knew not where to look for.

"I hope something tragic didn't happen to him." Jack said.

"No! Not again!" Enial exclaimed.

I remembered when Cezin had saved Witner's life and my promise to Briane to protect her brothers.

"We can't stay here and do nothing. We've got to find him where he is." Jack said to us.

"Where do we go?" I inquired.

"I don't know. We've got to do something, right?" Jack added.

"Our best bet is to call the cops and report him missing." I said, thinking I was smart.

"Not yet," Enial replied. "Was Witner over at his girlfriend's house? Did he go so far to Valparaizo for any reason? He was indeed going through rough times. I did not want to be so rude, but I also knew the odds were against us." We decided we should go over his girlfriend's home first and alert the police if he was not there.

When we arrived at the police station, the guard on duty greeted us rudely and soon we were under the impression that this ordeal was about to prolong.

"You came here looking for your brother and not one of you has identification?" He said to corner us.

"Is there a prisoner in here whose name is Witner?" I asked point blank.

"We don't know people by names. What does he look like?" He wanted to know.

"He's tall and skinny, sir." Enial said.

The officer handed us a book of prisoners' mug shots. Witner's photo was not in it.

"Our next option is to go to the office of the city medical examiner." I said.

"To do what? Find out if he's dead?" Enial said, terribly upset.

"Where is the medical examiner's office at?" Jack wanted to know.

I was not sure I got the address right and I did not want to keep talking about options.

When we got there, we saw a huge and tall man. He did not wear a uniform, as usual. He is out on a white tunic with a huge belt hanging low.

"Good morning. Are you a father or the caretaker of this place?"

"I am Father Amos. I have been coming to this place for years. And what can I do for you?"

"My friend, Witner, has been missing for three days. We wonder if he's here." I said.

"I saw him swimming in a pool of blood in the local hospital.

He was near death. Even though he was still alive, a crowd of gangs wanted to steal his body to ship abroad for experiment. You know what I mean. Do not put me in trouble. Anyhow, I prayed for him. That is what I do. I pray for patients at the hospital bed for years. This place has no caretaker. Volunteers clean up occasionally. This is no different from the General Hospital." He said firmly.

"Thank you, and so long" I said, wasting no time.

That was exactly where he had been. The intensive care unit was full. No empty beds for now, and there was no sign there would be one available soon. Witner, who had been bleeding for a while, was relieved to see us.

We asked for his release papers and took him to a nearby private clinic.

What happened was that every day he heard his brother's voice.

"Enial! Enial! Enial!" He screamed as soon as he was able to keep his eyes open.

He told us he was coming from a party at Sunny City late at night. He saw at the uppermost of a tree the same owl looking down at him. WE SAID IN UNISSON, "Are you serious Witner?" He responded, "Yes! I swear." He became so freaky. He lost his lucidity. And in three more blocks, he came across a score of mobs who demanded his wallet and his watch. By refusing to do so, he was knocked down unconsciously which incited me to shout, "Witner! Are your crazy brother?" I added,

"Take this lesson, any time you are in the middle of gang's situation, if you are asked to give up your wallet or anything valuable, you must surrender instantly. Gangs are merciless, cruel. They don't play." He said, "Got you."

He had scars on his face and forearm. And he was losing weight fast.

Unfortunately, a few weeks later, the doctor informed Enial that Witner died of concussion. And we immediately informed Briane what had happened.

"So far where the destiny takes me, I can imagine what is going on in Haiti," said Briane.

She succumbed but she dealt with it anyway. "But believe it or not, I am so defied, I can hardly eat. I hope you find a way to bury him. Give my regard to Kemal." She extolled back.

My sister Isabel and some previous Kitibel friends had to show their presence. They travelled so far from Valparaizo to Port-au-Prince to attend the funeral. There was no formal burial for Witner. Enial and Jack collected enough to pay for the coffin. Enial then carried the burden every day. He could hardly go anywhere or do anything without feeling Witner's presence. Obviously, he was deeply affected. His hope shattered. After a prolonged depression, he quit school and gave up sporting activities. How did he relate that to Briane so far in the foreign land?

"Sister, it's extremely hard for Jack and me to function properly, as you know. Now, we are broke. We look for work but as you know, we have no contact in the inner government circles. And I worry sick about this owl that showed up once before Witner died. I keep thinking everyday day, anytime, something similar can repeat itself again. Jack was dismissed from school for none progress. Our rent is far behind. If you can find a way to get us out here, please, let me know." Briane responded,

"I just want you to know I was thinking about this owl which triggered so many deaths in the family. I wonder, 'who will survive?' Even Cezin was not forgiven."

"Yes! I hear your cry. I feel deeply your pain back home. I live far away. I cannot mourn close to you to comfort you at this time of need. But I send you some cash that I accumulated from my part time job. Please manage it well until I will be able to do the same again. I will someday come back, and things will never be the same again. So long."

That was a five-page letter that described in detail what she thought Enial should do with the cash. He did not finish reading it. That he would do later, he convinced himself. He got some cash now. Just enough to get back on his feet—to move mountain, so to speak. It was a thousand dollars to be exact.

"How can we spend this wisely?" Jack asked, deep in thought.

"This is all we have. Rent is due again tomorrow. We got no food." Enial replied.

"You think of something and you know I'll be right by you." Jack said, in a flattering voice.

"What do you think of this? We sell the furniture, rent this place to somebody else, and go to Valparaizo." Enial said, convincingly.

"Valparaizo! We cannot live there. What's there to do?" Jack inquired.

"Yes, there is. I'll tell you if you let me finish," Enial replied.

"I'm not saying we're going to stay there. All I'm saying is we'll do exactly what Columbus did."

"I know what you're saying. Do you think we'll have enough?" Jack went on again.

"I already talked to a man that Colas referred me to. He wants two hundred dollars, but we'll work something out."

Enial and Jack arrived in Valparaizo at exactly 2 pm. This time, it was a long trip because the truck driver was incredibly old, Kitibel's former driver, and his vision is impaired. He did not remember them, nor did they introduce themselves. In fact, they did not even visit Kiti's former residence where they were born.

Soon they met a man in a strip club. He said his ship would leave the next day for Miami in VIRERON (illegal trip abroad).

"Follow me." He said.

Walking over the old rusty wharf, the man pointed at thirty feet silver boat. That was supposed to be the "kanter (tiny boat)." The word used to describe sailing to a foreign land.

"I believe you two are going. Give me the money now. I'll see you guys tomorrow."

Enial agreed but Jack hesitated.

"Briane is in New York. And we are here. I believe this curse on our mother that has manifested by this stupid owl is not a joke. If we stay here, we are going to die bro. Let us take a chance," Thought Enial.

The man left as soon as he pocketed the cash.

The next day, they arrived early. To their great surprise, folks were getting on a canoe—the silver boat was nowhere to be seen. They were about fifty-six persons, basically sitting on top of each other. That small, wooden thing weighted enough to carry seven. But before they even boarded Enial shouted loud enough to make everyone astonished, "Fuck! I cannot believe what I see flying above your boat captain. Everybody looks!" That was a twin black owl. Some people said,

"Don't worry kids they are just looking to make a catch. Fishes are all over the place." As Jack had tried to conceal the truth about the owl, Enial yelled, "What are we going to do Jacky?" "As far as I am concerned Enial, this is the last time we are going to see that. No more Owl's story when we reach Miami, our destination. No more," responded Jack.

Luckily, they sailed smoothly since the wind was blowing southwest. They saw hope and freedom ahead. They saw a better life coming. But, unfortunately, the canoe had sunk in Florida's deep water before Coast Guard arrived.

According to various press accounts, TV footage, and eyewitnesses, fifty-eight people were dead but the captain and a crew. They survived maybe to recount the story.

The news reached back home fast. Colas told me, both Enial and Jack were on that so-called boat, I cringed. I could not stop thinking of Briane. I was sort of surprised to get a letter from her:

"Pointless to reveal what happened to my brothers Kootan. That would be just to disrupt a broken heart. I already heard about it from the news. I am mourning alone presently. You are aware by now my life cannot be the same anymore. I probably need to watch this owl closely with me. The point is am I going to survive of this curse? All my people are gone, even Cezin. I dreamed about you every day. I feel you are indirectly next to me. I really want you to come over here."
She paused,

"Like many other couple, we can see the Harlem's renaissance together like we wish to rebuild Valparaizo or Haiti someday. It is like Sun City of Port-Au-Prince. There is Statue Liberty. It is a building made of iron. It stands for freedom and liberty for all. Once visitors walk in there, at the first sight they read, 'Give me your tired, your poor, your huddled masses yearning to breathe free. Send these, the homeless, tempest-tossed to me, I lift my lamp beside the golden door!'"
She continued,

"The city has the World Trade Center, which is a twin building, they are the tallest structure ever built in the world. But the city shares

ownership of these towers with New Jersey, the nationhood state. Indeed, Times Square'

All the activities of the city you name it take place in that vicinity. The famous one takes place on New Year's Eve. People travel from all over the world to come and see the ball dropping. Macys parade takes place on Thanksgiving Day has been remarkable as well. As you can see, I cannot wait to see you to share with me these experiences. Love you, Briane."

Was its coincidence or what? I just finished reading the letter when my sister, Isabel stopped by to congratulate me for having scored high in the national standardized test. I was on the top ten of my class. She knew that meant brilliance. Had I cheated on the test; she would have never known. She was proud of my accomplishment, and that was that. To her, I was just ready to continue our family legacy.

"What would you like?" She inquired.

I paused for a moment. When Isabel asked me a question like that, I already knew she would be getting me a nice gift. What it would be always depended on what my current need was. I smiled.

"Do you really want to know?" I shouted back.

"Yes, and I'm speaking on behalf of the entire family." She quipped.

"Help me get out of this country." I retorted.

"Are you nuts? Every day you hear how many people die on their way to Florida. Don't you listen to the radio? I'll be damned to let you sail a kanter."

The look on her face was an indication that she was serious. And the tone of her voice meant sympathy and concern.

"I wasn't talking about kanter, Isabel. I meant, flying. I'm asking you to help me get a visa."

She agreed on one condition: To enroll in engineering program and focus on getting a degree. But what I did not tell her was I would be going to see Briane. It would be fun.

"Find out how much I need to pay." She ordered me.

"I'll keep you informed. Remember, the sooner, the better," Said Isabel.

But I had a plan on my own. I already knew I had my aunt, Isabel's own sister who resided for many years in NYC. They never got along together. In addition to that, I had Briane to live with if bad comes to worse. I just stayed quiet.

I handed all my documents to Kitibel to work on it on her own way, my method did not count. In fact, I did not have to do anything. Unlike Briane with her Baptist Ministry, Isabel went to see father Bonenfant at The Catholic Parishioner to initiate everything for me. And within two months I received a package to travel to the city of New York to resume my studies. I already had a room and board, in addition to many engineering schools of my choice. I just had to contact them upon my arrival. Surprise!

Chapter VI

Reunion with Briane Abroad!

Surprisingly, Balthazar got me my scholarship. I joined Briane abroad, but what is a journey?

My plane landed smoothly at JFK International airport and began to disembark. While I remained buckled in my seat, I peered out in awe and was truly mesmerized. It was a bright sunny day during the winter season. I just had seen the city skylines before landing.

To me, that was a new world, a new beginning as I boarded on my long journey in a foreign land. Except for only one thing, I was not quite sure if I had been followed by the owl that took Kitibel to her tomb. Yes, that was possible because I was too much involved in the family, especially Briane. Yes, I was the last passenger to get off. I stumbled a bit as I walked down the aisle, and feverishly greeted everyone in sight. I found the airport huge and clean, which was quite the opposite of where I had boarded. Also, the agents were friendly and helpful—something I was not accustomed to see and I was not prepared for. I was expecting to be scrutinized and thoroughly searched if any suspicion arose. None of that happened, thank God. Everything went smoothly and that concerned me deeply. I had heard many times how immigration agents could be ruthless and would hesitate to detain me. To escape them I would have to come correct, and that was what I did.

"Where do I go from here?" I mumbled to myself.

I had written a long letter to Briane informing her of my trip and requested that she pick me up if she had the time. I had not heard back from her on time, but I was hoping she would be here.

I was a world away and my enthusiasm was far from being dampened. Wondering aimlessly and clutching my throat, I was relieved to see a young lady sprinting towards me and as soon as I realized it was Briane, I restrained myself not to burst into tears.

She looked great. In fact, she was now a full-grown woman with its pointing like a scud missile and, her eyes sparkling. Whatever lipstick she used succeeded in making the point. I rolled off my suitcase just in time as she hugged me, which was quite an emotional appeal of significance.

"Welcome to the Big Apple!" She whispered in my ear.

I had not heard that term before, but I knew what she meant. We were both happily surprised to see each other, knowing we could be a strong couple. At least, that was what

I was thinking. I had been there for her, already expressed my love and gratitude, and what not.

She reminded me of my teenage years, of course. The way I looked at it now, she was my last and best female friend and, I sum, she reflected the folks we both had grown up with. Folks like Debora, Helena, my aunt, the famous dog Cezin, and of course her three brothers: Enial, Jack and Witner. I told her I was supposed to go to the Catholic Parishioner at St. Patrick Cathedral because I was expected there. But I did not really want to go there, and they could not care less if I did not show up. Who really wanted to oversee youngsters knowing what the leaders and officials were going through with them? For my case, I was afraid of repeating the past. I did not want to see myself in the same situation as I was growing up when I had to wake up at ungodly hours to serve as an altar boy. I explained to Briane my situation hoping she would share the burden with me.

She convinced me not to go to this place. She also remembered the old days and what I used to go through. While every single kid stayed in bed, I would be singled out to join priests to serve as altar boy. And I surely did listen to her. But the real burden for me was that my aunt was expecting me. That was the plan B in case I was not welcome in the monastery.

"Would you please give this to the cab driver?" I inquired, as I passed her a note. It was my aunt's address supposedly. She paused for a second, evidently noticed something was amiss. She convinced me there was no such address and I believed her. I might have jotted it down in hurry, for all I knew. I found myself in a quandary because I surely knew my aunt, a woman I never met, was expecting me but I would not want her to be alarmed if I did not show up. My list of friends in the city was not long; in fact, none I could stay with.

Would Briane appreciate my blunt honesty? Ah, she did not let me tell it, even after we hopped in a yellow cab. I just saw plenty of them in front of the terminal.

Our driver was somewhat cordial but had the decency to turn down the loud reggae song he was listening to.

"What have you been doing with yourself?" I asked her.

"The usual. Work and go to school. More work, more school. That's pretty much it."

"Yeah, I can only imagine. You don't seem to be complaining." I said.

"I wouldn't get anything out of it if I did. I know what my goal is." She interjected.

In a brief flash, I noticed she was certainly ambitious but her mangle. And I also knew that eventually I would drag it all out of her.

Suddenly, the driver pulled up in front of a building in the upper west side, or Washington Heights to be exact. I did what he asked me to, I hopped out and rang the bell.

As the cab rolled away, I waved goodbye at Briane, who was on her way to school.

My aunt buzzed me in. The world got nothing on me yet. I spent the next several days inside the tiny apartment, pretty much talking to Briane on the phone late at night when I was feeling crushed by insomnia.

So far, auntie Islande had been good to me. She let me eat her food. No problem. She even left breakfast on the stove for me.

The kitchen was so small it could hardly fit two people. Its floor is creaky, its plastic tiles peeled off.

Islande was not young but not old enough to retire. She went to work every day, and when she came home, she would tell me how she hated her commute, how fearful she was of teenage gangs, and how she took pains in dismissing panhandlers. She would rant about the sidewalks being taken over by illegal street vendors—from whom she bought cheap winter gloves and umbrella.

We lived up on the top floor of the building, so through my room windows I would watch intently what was happening on the street. And there was a lot of it. How was this any different from what I had earlier witnessed in Haiti?

The similarities were obvious, but here in New York, I was not yet part of it. I was now determined that would not last long. I had enough of staying home, watching morning soap operas on television, and ate her food. My greatest surprise was after so much effort to relocate to USA for my education my scholarship had been either cancelled or postponed for the following semester. The main reason for it is because I failed to present to the monastery at my arrival to pick up the package. It was believed that I did make it to the USA, so it was either cancelled or postponed. So, I was put in a waiting list for the following semester upon demand.

I was immensely fighting within myself to find a way to get out of this confinement. Meanwhile, I studied English all alone and the dusty books on the lamp table were proof of my effort. I learned fast. Not only I had to keep up with Briane but also, I ought to be prepared to begin my engineering program. But "How in the world am I going to get the money to pay for my tuition since my scholarship has not been ready yet?" I thought.

Decidedly, I wrote Isabel,

"Forgive me sister for being so late to inform you with my whereabouts. Now let me tell you how things came along for me in my new home. First, aunty Islande welcomed me with open arms so did Briane, including the monastery. But forgive me Sis but I have decided to not join the latter because New York's way of living demands that I changed my plan. For instances, I will have to get home on time and restricted to bring friends there. So, I choose to stay with aunty Islande. Please, I beg you to support me for room and board while I will continue to use my award for books and tuition. Now, I will do my best to earn my diploma because someday I shall return to recoup for you all the lost. I terminate hoping this will make you feel better at this point. Islande, Briane, and I salute you cordially. Love you, Kootan."

One month later, Isabel answered me back. She showed a lot of sympathies in her correspondences for me than what I anticipated. And that was very encouraging to me. Now, I saw no obstructions for me not to begin my studies.

As soon as I resumed classes for the semester, Briane's intention was not so pure. She wanted me to put my studies on the side and begin to wander around looking for adventure or anything else. I said,

"Briane, I should give priority to my studies first before anything else instead. My presence here costs Kiti an arm and a leg, this is her bloody money. I must use it for the purpose intended. Even though I have not admitted to the University yet, I can use part of the money to study English at least in a private institution. Besides, Briane you already had your two years of education toward your goal and me, none. Please, promise me you won't ask me for that again?"

On the following day, Briane surprised me one morning. She insisted to take a trip to the Statue of Liberty. It was her day off, so she chose a place she had not yet been to. She did not ask me what I thought or if I had another idea. Not that it would have mattered any way.

"You did not come just to stay home only. There are so many things you can enjoy as learning. Let brake out," insisted Briane. I thought she had a point and if I had not complied with her demand, she would drive me crazy. Decidedly, I said, "I agree to mix pleasure with my education if you don't mind seeing me with books while I accompany you in the train." She responded, "I surely won't challenge you because in number II train, almost everyone carries either a book or newspaper." I said, "Okay Briane, you got it!"

We were waiting at the underground station for almost an hour before the train arrived. There was a delay, but the booth clerk did not bother to make any such announcement.

We smelled something outrageously funky as soon as we boarded the number II train. There were lots of empty seats, which was rather unusual, she observed. A pushcart filled with beer can bottles, old rags, and cardboards, was at the other end.

"Where is he going with all that stuff?" I inquired.

"Nowhere. He's home now." She said, pinching her nose. "He's such a young man too. Look at him. That is what he chooses to do, of all things."

Thank God, we switched cars. She was getting a little bit overheated, and even more so when a beggar standing next to us began singing a Christmas Carol.

I was still baffled. I did not think it was at all possible there would be common folks living in this great city in such a sorry state. Did they prefer it that way?

I was thinking I could also be unfair or biased. Perhaps it reminded me of Sun City.

We did get lost, but we arrived safely at the South Ferry station.

As we waited to get aboard the ferry, I whispered in her ear.

"This is a big kanter."

"Except no one got to pay a dime." She added, while laughing.

"I can't believe I'm actually going to see the statue. I read a bit about it, its rich history, and so forth. But now I can really touch it. Amazing, isn't it?"

"Yes, it is. Do you know what it stands for?"

"Don't be ridiculous. Any fifth-grader would know that."

A Family in Shambles!

"Just tell me."

"Ah, now I see what you're doing. You are testing me. All right, since that's what you're doing, I am happy to tell you it stands for freedom to all the immigrants who reach the shore".

"It was a gift from the French people." She added quickly in her thick accent.

"But I wouldn't call it a gift. Why? Because Michel Bartholdi got commissioned by an American financier to build it, and that same man paid to have it shipped to the shore." I said.

We snapped pictures and carried on about the size of that humongous statue. The tour ended rather nicely. We made plan to return, hopefully in a warm weather. We hugged before we parted ways.

Finally, the long-awaited summer arrived! Ah, what a relief it was, I hang up my coat. Moreover, I was determined to find a job or do something, whatever it was, to bring in some cash. Time was running out, hardship quietly settling in. I could not rely only on Isabel so in Valparaizo. So, I no longer feared street gangster, I was not going to allow myself to be worried about that. I used to gang back home. I had a few kinks to work on, all but pressing.

I began to look at my options. Truthfully, there were not too many. I would not dare ask Islande to buy me the things I needed. Or anything, for that matter! That, understandably, was not part of the arrangement. Besides, I was a grown man. I should have been taking care of her.

121

What worried me most was my legal status. I was here on a student visa, but I got to work. The more I thought about it, the more depressed I became. It felt as though I had a mountain of ice to break.

I shared my concern with my aunt, who laid out a perfect plan.

"Find out how much it costs to have a gypsy cab." She said.

"I'll let you know tomorrow. I'll have to call an insurance broker and get a quote." I replied.

"I'm sure you'll take it from there."

"Thank you for your offer. I want you to know I will repay you the money as soon as I can. You got my word."

"Stop it, young man."

I obeyed. Circumstances got me into this mess, devotion got to get me out. I got my driver's license, bought, and insured a used car, and hit the street without proper inspection.

My first day as a cab driver was more experimental than anything else. Slowly driving around with a city map, I tried to remember the names of the main avenues and popular streets.

I drove mostly in Harlem, where I figured I was going to make my daily bread. Right in the heart of the city, mind you. Both attractive and unattractive in its own way, it offered me the opportunity to judge and compare. What I quickly found out was that the city was more segregated than it appeared. Going through the western and central parts of Harlem was more troublesome than exciting.

To say both parts were heavily black would not be inaccurate. Harlem is filled with vacant lots and rundown buildings. It is also filled with churches big and small of all denominations, and scores of funerals room. And that was just the tip of the iceberg. The main thoroughfares looked quite the same. The bodega occupied the corner, the liquor store right in the middle of the block, and the funeral homes not too far from the church. Everything seemed isolated and delineated, and it became a way of life.

What I saw on the side streets were more compelling than what I had heard. It was not uncommon to hear gunshots coming out of the residential at broad daylight, as well as the whirring of a police car chasing the gunman.

With equal clairvoyance, I noticed that most young men standing on the street corners had fewer front teeth, but they loved to laugh loud at their own jokes and shout out at their peers while the street preachers would not mind spilling out their Gospels.

The older men, those who liked to throw wood logs and newspapers into a metal bin and set it on fire to stay warm, were not fallen angels. They would hardly beg, and if they did, it would be mostly nickeling and dimes to complete the booze's money. Cheap liquor was shared among them. Too much of it made them looked sick, aged, and paralyzed. There was, too, something else ravaging their heart and soul. The epidemic heroin, an axis of evil!

How these inoffensive people lived and what they went through to just barely maintain their stock created a few wrinkles on my forehead. What in God's name was going on? Teenage pregnancy was on the rise, lots of baby strollers being pushed. Some of them turned out to be good parents, whether they lived in shelters or not. Law-abiding citizens they were. They hoped someday their kids—at least one of them—would fare better and, if that ever happened, that would bring financial relief and social togetherness to the family. And much respect.

I had another guest coming. I was taking a passenger to a local hospital on the upper Westside when I began to realize this side of town was completely different than I was getting used to. In every way imaginable! The streets were clean, the buildings stunning.

Guards on foot patrolled the area. Police officers maintained a solid presence. What was that all about? Well, for one thing, that was where the do-gooders lived, and they were white.

The tale of two sections within a city, one embraced me and the other ignored me.

The very first time I drove my aunt to church, she had me cracked up. Gossips and tidbits were flying high. I was now behaving like a normal driver. And that seemed to make her happy. Not really. She was happy that I kept my word so far, that I was able to pay some bills.

"Come to church with me some day and I'll introduce you to a nice girl. I know her parents. Her mom and I are tight."

"I will go one day. I missed going to church. But it won't be for her." I replied.

"Once you meet her, you'll be going to my church every time. You won't even wait for me to get ready."

"Auntie, I must confess I have strong feelings for Briane. I have always been in love with her. I think I should ask her to marry me. Tell me what you think?" I said

She cackled. She already knew. She was just waiting to hear it from me.

"I can't tell a grown man what to do and I don't stick my nose into other people's business. That is not me. But since you asked, I will say this, do not rush. You don't know her that well." She said.

"I am not rushing it. I know her very well. That's Kitibel's daughter."

"I know that. My take on it is, she has been here for two years and you just got here. You do not know what she has been up to. Bet she's not telling you everything." She added furiously.

I was slightly surprised she had no great liking for Briane. I just had a bite of it. I listened with fascination, and any perceptible nuance caught my attention.

I put on the brakes in the church's parking lot and, in my own ghastly way, let her out.

I sat there for a moment, thinking. I had a problem, but not one I felt particularly inclined to ignore.

I thought I would slave my guts out, and hopefully get something good out of it.

It was a hot day and I had difficulty getting in touch with Briane, so I figured I could be making money instead of being emotionally drained. Pouch under the eyes. Jumpy I was. The curtain was dropped.

I worked long hours that day and well into the night. Though I remained focused, my eyes were blurry. I often shifted my weight to roll down the window so I could have a clear view of anyone hailing a cab.

I was not doing an exhibition. I was exhausted. I decided that recent to me and, before I knew it or said a word, two others hopped in. They all got comfortable and ordered me to keep driving.

"Where ya gwan, brethrens?" I asked, faking a Jamaican accent.

"Don't worry about where we're going. We'll let you know when we get there." One said.

"This nigger ain't from here, y'all." Shouted another one. "He might be using fake license and stuff."

I did a good job at concealing my fear and took enough care to skirt danger. Immediately afterward, they rolled a joint, which I believed was marijuana. I was told to blast the radio and kept the windows locked. The stinky smell invaded as they puffed and shared the weed as a common right. These were not Zingas by any means. They appeared to have become fixated on me. I was looking for a way out. I decided what I was going to do and how I was going to do it if I ran into a police car. That was all mental speculation, steamed coffee without napkin. The nonsense took a different turn when the youngest one rested his stinky left foot on the back of my seat. I rolled down the window and stick my head out, gasping for fresh air. I thought about Father Bonenfant. I enunciated the two psalms of David, 23 and 91 immediately. That is what I always used in front of adversity. Now I shouted,

"Why am I not surprised? Do you know where you are going? Is that how you live your life, for real?" I said, in a defiant tone,

"Nigger shut the hell up. We do not wanna hear crap from you. Heard?"

The same boy uttered, "Make me."

I bristled, as I tucked my hand inside my jacket's pocket. They did not know for sure if I had a gun but, lo and behold, that was not a piece of jewelry. I took risk in doing that. It eclipsed all faint shadow. I had no interest in knowing what they were about, but I sensed they needed a new infusion of schooling to carry them in life. I would have mentioned a few things about street gang violence and that would have been appropriate. I would have shed some light on black history. Or their ancestors, for that matter! I was certain they would not want to be engaged in how we black ended up in this country. They were quick to call me an immigrant, no doubt.

Did they know they were sons of former immigrants? Of course, they would have asked me what the hell I was saying.

"I left home to come here because I was on the run. See, let me share this with y'all. Two teenagers tried to rob me off my money in Haiti. And you wanna know what I did. I shot them." I said.

My bluff and lie worked on my favor, so it seemed. In some ways, these young men were easy to deal with. They hopped out when I stopped at a traffic light.

"This is my hood too, you know. This is where I make my money.

So, I'm sure I'll see you guys again." I said. I was heading home, all flustered. I thought of my relatives back in Valparaizo, my sister Isabel. I expedited a package full of pens, notebooks, and rulers. It was not much, but that is all I could afford. I figured out she would help the downtrodden greatly before the school opened. But, after these incidents I realized I could have been dead and, started wondering, "Was it really the reason why I came to this country? Or to get myself killed?"

The next morning was all bad news. When I explained to Briane what happened, she yelled, "Kootan you need a good luck bathe. You should not vehiculate like a chicken like that. This world is too dangerous. Yes! You need take a bathe for protection."

"My faith had been in God in the middle of all of that. ...In fact, I did call him and, He immediately rescued me..." I alleged.

The next morning, I found my car's tires slashed. All four. The back windows shattered, and the backlights all broken. Someone, or perhaps a group of three, might have been in a volcano of rag. One good news was, surprisingly, I received my scholarship to report to the City University of New York immediately to resume my studying. I was stunned and full of joy.

"If Briane is about to get her diploma, what about me?"

I thought I should focus on my education to catch up with her. So, I wasted no time.

CHAPTER VII

Education and Graduation

The following day Briane gathered some friends of similar faith to do some mazonzon (voodoo charms) on my behalf. I could not tell if I was really protected. But even though I did in what way! My God had always been there for me. I needed no protection from no loas. And when I learned about what Briane did, I was very furious about it.

I dropped the car at a nearby mechanic shop and, I went straight to the police station to report the incident. Aftermath, I debuted on Briane at the entrance of the University, as I had carried my acceptance letter and scholarship with me. She was so thrilled to see my documents. She guided me from A to Z on the registration process. Everything went so well for me.

I met indeed with a counselor, a heavyset woman who did more preaching than counseling. But I was not about to let anyone discourage me from taking more classes. Neither she nor Briane stood a chance because the letter stipulated to study civil engineering. I surely did. The window of opportunity was at the time. Reassuringly much anticipated.

Besides, I had to be a full-time student to be qualified for a lot of goodies, one of which is being able to live on campus. The place I wanted to be, the place I needed to be. But even though I did get these scholarships I was very prepared to meet any challenge that came across. First, as soon as I set foot on this country, I secured myself financially.

Briane was not paying attention when we left the building and walked towards a bookstore nearby. She kept twisting her hair and cramming it onto her back, something she would do when upset.

If I had asked what was troubling her, she would be in denial. I grabbed her book bag and slugged it over my shoulders.

"What are you doing? Give this back to me." She said.

"I'm getting one just like yours. Cute, isn't it?" I stammered.

"Not a pink one, I'll tell you that much." She inferred,

"Do you like me?" I asked.

"Don't be silly. Of course, I like you." She replied.

"Would you like to be my girlfriend?" I asked.

"I'll have to see about that. We are not going to have much time to see each other. I am busy day and night. You, too, are going to be terribly busy." She said.

"That will be temporary. Besides, you do not want me to be all over you. You said so yourself." I thought.

"Yes, I did. And you want to know why? Because you are a jealous man and that is what you are. You are sweet and everything. But your jealousy, boy, it's been off the hook." She said.

It felt as though she had just set me on fire. The devil was testing me on all fronts. But then again, why wouldn't I be jealous? Any man who knew her as much as I did would. An undeniable fact whether she wanted to admit it or not.

"Are you referring to the incident with Kemal?" I inquired.

"That too was uncalled for. You gave that boy hell for no damn reason." She quipped.

"I never understood what was going on between you two. That made me concerned." I said.

"You were my friend until my brothers, and I moved to Port-au-Prince. You were not there for me, Kootan. You were still back in Valparaizo. So, let me tell you how it all happened because that is something, I have always wanted to get off my chest. I was dating Kemal casually at first. I was waiting on you to ask me out, but you never did." She uttered.

I stood in dismay, engulfed by true sadness. I got caught unprotected, sweating and all. Truth be told, I had not liked Kemal, a scavenger to me. Though I was blamed for the outcome, I nonetheless felt betrayed and heartbroken and her repentance did not soothe my jealousy.

"I admit I was wrong. I'm asking you out now." I said, flatteringly.

She stifled a cough, shook her head, and parted her lips—all in that order.

"What must I do to convince you to go out with me next weekend?" I asked.

"Stop the wind from blowing on my face." She said.

She kissed me on the cheek before she took the train on the way to work. Yes, she was going to work, and I was not. I desperately needed a job. That much was certain.

My actions would have to overcome consequences. A new reality began to dawn on me.

Going to school afforded me the honor to meet my fellow countrymen and other students from all walks of life. There were plenty. The fact that I was going to seminars, lectures, and workshops, I casually befriended some of them, mostly those in their senior years. I was only trying to keep up, and often argue, with them. My attention was always stern, welcoming a bout. I would not speak too soon nor be distracted by vernacular spills. Too cautious to be tangled in the net! Sure, that was my strategy, all right.

No point in being a show-off, even in the haste of the moment.

I was in the cafeteria and, while waiting for my meaty sandwich to be hot, I bumped into a former professor of mine. A tall, languid man with broad shoulders and bulging forearms, he could hardly be unnoticed.

"What a surprise to see you here Professor Poneau?" I said quickly in Creole.

He did not bother to respond, although outwardly he tried to show remarkable humility. He soon joined me at the table and shook my hand.

"You must be Kootan, right?" he asked.

Of course, he knew my name. I was not flashing my student ID, nor was he entirely dismissal of my attempt. He simply did not want to engage me in Creole. Why not? A shame, it was. He hated being ridiculed for his accent, his culture, and customs. Or so he claimed.

"Are you visiting or teaching a class?" I asked.

"None, I'm a student just like you." He replied.

"Really? Oh, that is fantastic. What's your major?" I asked.

"I just took a few classes to complete my degree in Architectural Design! I'll be out next semester."

"Any job offers, yet?" I implored, a bit excitedly.

"They hardly hire someone my age for an entry-level job. I do not care much, anyway. I keep doing what I'm doing now, save some money, and go back home."

Confusion tapped in. He, who had taught me the very basics of algebra and geometry, was now in a bottom-of-the-barrel predicament.

So were many others his age, so were many others his looks. He was not counting on the donkey for a free ride or on the bull for crumb. He could care less about reaping the benefits of retirement and health insurance. He never got seriously ill, though.

He was going to use his training where it mattered most, where he was known as a Professor. I wished him luck. I too needed luck and prayers because I was going nonstop. I hardly rested my body and that would soon begin to take a toll on me. Fatigue was chronic. Fever lasted longer than usual.

It was not until a few days before Christmas that my energy returned to normal level like a bunny in a well-kept barnyard.

Thanks to Islande. Although I had run two miles a day and been at the gym regularly, I had not gotten better until Islande cured me with her own medicine. No, it was not the pills from her cabinet. Rather she cooked a stew made with cow foot, spinach, and watercress. That was my breakfast, lunch, and dinner for a week.

"This is just like Kitibel Special." I said, in a congratulatory tone.

"This taste much better than what she used to make. Unlike her, I didn't use much salt and hot pepper." She said, smiling.

"You're absolutely correct." I replied.

"If I had the money, I would open a restaurant. You'd be the chef." I added.

"I'm flattered. But I do not think we would be making a profit, though." She bemused.

"You've got to be kidding me. Your food is, how should I put it? Delicious." I said.

"Here's what you don't understand, Kootan. It takes time to prepare and cook a delicious meal. And it's expensive." She boasted.

As almost always, she was right on the money. But I also remembered Kitibel had in fact been successful in her endeavor and idolized by some young women in Valparaizo. Whatever my aunt or I now thought of Kitibel's cooking style had no merit.

And it would have been synthesizing hypocrisy since I had very much enjoyed the "Special".

"I got news for you. Kitibel never actually cooked. It was always the maids. But they never got credit for it."

"True. Both Helena and Debora helped." I added.

"Please, she was too busy doing other things, if you know what I mean." She said.

"Any way, she left the kids with a good deal of cash and a big house in Haiti." I uttered.

"Mayor Turenne was getting bribed by the drug lords, so he gave Kitibel some money for the house when his wife found out he was having an affair. It wasn't money she made from the restaurant, my dear." She added.

What a disturbing revelation! The disapproving looks on Islande's eyes troubled me even more, but I was so composed she could not take me amiss. I did not dare question her reasoning, there was no reason to, and there lay my mistake.

"What has become of Turenne, you know?" I inquired

"He died. His oldest son Turenne II became the new mayor of Valparaizo. You didn't know?" she asked.

"Really? What of it?"

"Some say he is still living and stay forever young, which I don't believe is true. Others say he suffers with hernia. When I went to Valparaizo years ago, I do not remember exactly, he was bed-ridden with that hernia. I was told his hernia was acting up. And he was home alone."

"Where was his wife?"

"Well, she finally divorced him. Where were his mistresses? Well, he was broke, so they must have fled." She said, without a pause.

I was sent to get some hot tea, and in doing so, I took longer just to avoid her unleashing. And to get further away from her, I started to fix the water leak underneath the sink.

A minor type of work, but I had been procrastinating. She did not bother asking me to do it. I was not a plumber. But, as a man with a formal Boy Scout training, I should have been able to stop the leak or, at the very least, gotten the building's superintendent in.

How about that big container in the hallway?

It was my obligation to take that to a man, a self-proclaimed exporter of goods, who would ship it to Valparaizo. Islande had been using him for years, with truly little problem. And I knew that container was heavy, half the things were dry food cans. The other half was—guess what—a pile of garbage bags filled with used clothes.

I had some difficulty in getting in touch with that man, but when I finally did, he conned me into paying more per weight, saying repeatedly that the price for "everything" went up. Like what? The cargo boat increased its fee when the gas price jumped. So did the truck drivers. Oh, there was the domino effect. He got higher bills to pay and his Jewish landlord was threatening to have his lease revoked.

Such was life in the city. We made it even more complex. Islande was now a New Yorker. So was that conniving disgruntled exporter.

Did I ever become a New Yorker?

Yes, in hope and lifestyle! No, in heart and culture!

Fast forward, I would be as clear as a crystal ball. A turning point in my life, a feeling of accomplishment would overwhelm me.

All that and more were a culmination of years of hard work and school, all with care and diligence. I pursued my dream relentlessly. I pledged to make a difference.

Five years later, on the very same date I had arrived in New York, I attended Briane's graduation commencement. I was thrilled she graduated summa cum laude, the result of her devotion.

With diploma in hand, she held me by the waist side. We kissed every time we held each other tight.

Sometimes eye-teary, sometimes bustling with joy, she thanked me for being there whenever she needed me during those school years. A boyfriend, she could count on.

"Out of respect, I shall call you Dr. Briane," I said.

"Hey Kootan!" responded this girl, "That is not what I am thinking presently," pouring tears which seemed to be unstoppable. "I am thinking about my Mom Kitibel, my brothers, Helena, and Debora and of course, Cezin would have sniffed me all over the place."

"Yes, I'm Dr. Briane. And Mr. Kootan is my first patient." She said, laughing.

"Well, where's the bed, doctor?" I replied.

"I never said you were admitted."

She banged me in the head, while I tried to hide my face with my overcoat. This was how she expressed her joy on occasion.

"Well! This is a time to enjoy, not to be sad, BB." I hissed though. She just smiled, "You have a point Kootan."

Things seemed to be happening the way she had planned them. She did her residency at a well-respected hospital where she would later be hired. Specialized special diseases so she would tend to people's needs and more importantly done with school. She only spent one year at that hospital. But the most important, she grabbed that circumstance to make lot of friends. She thought someday she might need them back home to help cure various diseases that terrified her fellow human beings.

How in God's name did she do all that?

She had no shame in telling me she had lived on borrowed money, which she intended to repay. So, what? She had done what she had to do. Her decision to become a doctor had been made, so what was there for me to worry about? Nothing but my own damn self!

What did I do?

I graduated a few months later. Now I became a civil engineer. I got my degree to prove it. Unlike Briane, I got no real job offer but I was able to line up a few prospects. Besides, we were now engaged—unofficially. It was our understanding if I became successful in convincing her to renounce to voodoo, I would marry her. The time would tell. But l replicated the same technic Briane had used in staying friendly with many classmates as possible for later use in Haiti. And since I have no job offer, I said to myself, "Maybe it is the time to think about Haiti, especially Valparaizo. I believed I could be especially useful for my people. A la maison!

Chapter VIII

Home Return

The next morning, I made my way to the Consulate to get my passport renewed. I ran into Poneau who happened to be at my school for the same reason to acquire an engineering degree and go back home. He informed me that our government was looking to hire a few engineers and medical doctors for some new national projects. Valparaizo had been included in them. He gave me all the proper contacts and agreed I could use him as reference. Cool! I asked, "How much am I going have as entry level?"

"It's not how much you get paid, Kootan. It is how much more you can make in that position. That is what it is. That is how you must look at it. It's called…" said Poneau.

"Yeah! That's what it is." I replied.

"Exactly. As I can see, you get my drift. I hope I'll see you back home." He added.

"I'll need to find out what the project is and make my decision from that." I said.

He laughed.

"Why do you care? It is not like you have any experience, but I agree it is time for you to put your theories into practice. Think about that." He said, before he hopped on a yellow cab.

Of course, I would need time to think it over, investigate the project thoroughly, and—here is the crux of the matter—discuss its entirety with Dr. Briane.

She and I had been spending more time together, the seed of our love. I would meet her during her lunch break in a nearby fancy but relatively inexpensive restaurant where we would intelligently and talk about whatever made the headline news of the local papers. I respected her opinion, she respected mine.

Sometimes, we would meet after work and do something remarkably fun—like going to see Safarina on Broadway or pay a visit to the Museum of Modern Art. On weekends, we would drive up north and enjoy:

The scenery of an isolated place!

The cattle farm in a place that stood to attention! The trees on their own recess! The cottages and their accoutrement!

Time afforded us to be sympathetic and loyal to each other.

The connection between us grew synergistically.

I was a changed man, notorious for my distinguished manners and intellectual impulses but fearful of social humiliations and failures. Briane had already concluded I was in a crazy state of mind. Her way of saying I was nerdy.

Social life seemed to occupy us entirely. A week or so later, on New Year's Eve, we went out on a date, if you could call it that. We went to Times Square to witness the famous celebration of the ball dropping from the sky. Although we had rushed to get there early, we found ourselves mesmerized or discomforted by what we saw going on right before our eyes, worse yet, right before the cops. There was a heavy presence of pimps and hookers. Neon signs at porn movie theaters and X-rated video stores flickered. Beggars and comedians blended in. Movers and shakers strode by, and lards rolled in aggressively.

There were, too, a lot of tourists—some looked easy prey to the professional thieves and others overpaid for knockoff watches and gadgets. All that and more were the main attraction.

"You won't believe what I'm about to tell you." I said, attempting to divert her attention.

"Don't tell me then." She replied.

I looked away and seemed immersed in the traffic, noticing how many cabs went through the red light and, in so doing, they came close to hitting pedestrians.

"What is it?" She now wanted to know.

"Our government has offered me a job, an exciting position, really." I said.

"Congratulations. What exactly will you be doing?" She asked.

"I'm told the job will be based in Valparaizo where I'll oversee building roads that will connect the counties. I don't know much about the project, and no one is providing me more details until I get to Port-Au-Prince, Haiti." I replied. I also expressed that was our goal, to come back someday to Valparaizo to change it for the better.

"Don't rush. That is all I can tell you. As you know, a career in our government is not a sure thing. Go there and see what the offer is all about before you commit." She said, pessimistically.

"I'd like you to come with me." I said, staring at her.

"How nice of you to ask but that's something I'll have to think through." She replied.

"We'll get married in our hometown and you won't have to work." I said.

"I didn't go to medical school to become a housewife." She said.

We decided to leave New York City environment as we explored every single digit of opportunity, we could get there. We kissed this milk and honey land and said goodbye like the ball dropped at Times Square for the new year.

We boarded the airplane to Haiti. Then I thought that was funny, I shouted to Briane, "We forget to pick up something dearly to us," Briane inquired, "What is it Baby?"

"Your famous Owl." Briane infuriated. I hugged her very tight.

After so many years of absence, we survived. We acquired the maximum of it with medical and engineering degrees. I screeched, "Briane! The Owl must be very stupid, she could not even figure out how to mess up with the differential equation and, of course your complex form of human diseases in our curricula." She shouted, "I believed he's broke, he could not make it to New York City. He would not find fund for the airplane ticket. Besides, Papa Damballa had always been there for me." I yelled,

"Oh no, Briane! That was really Father Bon's prayer. What about the psalms 23 and 91? They had no effect at all?" We thought that was funny, we just joked about it. And that was it.

In a sweltering heat that could take human lives, Briane and I rushed out of the airport in Port-Au-Prince, Haiti after an exceptional fly.

We were afraid we would be begged for cash and worried about getting sick, but home should be home. We would find a way to deal with it. I felt dehydrated and my appetite gone. She, on the other hand, was tensed. She put aside her luggage and looked up. Oh my God, she had never seen this before and might not have moved from that spot had I not encouraged her to come along. So many scary-looking young men walk by bare-chested and muttered to themselves as they scanned the area for newcomers. Hustlers and con artists shouted obscenity and senseless self-hate. The road was unsanitary, and the pebble of the garbage bank was quite an eyesore. She looked back over her shoulder, not long enough to conceal her edginess.

I hovered endlessly at her side. To us, this was flux and a painful reminder. Our human psyche must have fallen asleep or idled great energy saved. But we threaded our way, hopped on a hoop tie, and ordered the driver to leave the scene hurriedly. It is easier to say than the ill-shaven driver was so furious he almost hit every beggar that got on the way, literally. Then, he sped up, honking, and passing every other vehicle on the road. He did not talk to us nor bother asking us where we were going. For a brief second, Briane would confess to me later, she thought we were being kidnapped.

When he finally slowed down, he was pulling in the parking lot of a fancy hotel—the most talked-about hotel among visiting Haiti. How did he know we were staying there?

Well, for one thing, we looked and smelled different. We had an air of great importance, all basked in glow.

"How much I owe you, sir?" I asked.

He waited. He had no meter, so he would have to think about it. While he was still undecided, I took the opportunity to check in and get change at the concierge. I left Briane at the lobby, went outside and paid him.

"I was waiting to see if you'd remember me," he said, standing like a fool he was.

We shook hands. I just realized it was Colas, though he looked older than he was. I had not seen him in over half a decade and never heard about him either.

"Was that Briane with you?" he continued.

"Yes, you sure remember her, don't you?" I said.

"I sure do." He added.

"Wait. Colas, you mean to tell me you knew it was me in the back seat and you said nothing." I demanded a full explanation.

"I didn't know how you would react. People from the Diaspora act funny sometimes. You know, like they are superior and all that. Anyway, welcome back old friend." He said.

We kicked each other's left leg and bellowed shouts of cry—something we had fraternized as Boy Scouts. No, it was not hostility or barbaric transgression. We just disentangled the syllabus and thus rekindled our boyhood days in Valparaizo.

"Thank you. It feels good to be back here." I answered in a low voice.

"How long will you guys be here?" He implored.

"You mean, here at the hotel?" I shouted back.

"Yeah that too." He continued.

"Just for the weekend, but if you want to know how long we'll be staying in Haiti, I don't have an answer for that." I said.

"Did you go to school in New York?" he asked.

"I sure did. I am an engineer. I am here to see what I can do to make some tremendous improvements. How about you?" I said.

He pointed at the car, kicked the tires, and grew red.

"This is what I do to make a buck. I'm ashamed of it, but that's all I got to feed my kids."

"How many kids do you have?" I interrupted.

"A twin girl with my first wife and two boys with my second wife." He continued, "How about you?"

"No kids yet, but I'm working on it." I uttered.

I advanced, "But you've been too fast Colas. I hope you stop right there. I've been out only for five years plus and you're telling me you engender three kids."

We thought that was funny. We laughed about it and we figured we had a lot of catching up to do and thus, we postponed it at a later day. Now I had to tend to my fiancée, and I did not want her to be in a state of panic—which would have been quite alright since we just arrived in a land where law-abiding citizens got lost without a trace or killed. Besides, I was tired and needed to take a nap.

"Are you going to rent a car?" he asked deliberately.

"I was going to. But why would I do that? You're here now." I replied.

"My car is your car, buddy." He said.

I took his number and went upstairs to my room where I caught Briane looking out of the window.

"Who was that?" she asked.

"You wouldn't believe it was my friend Colas. Remember him?" I said.

If she had answered me, I did not recall. I showered and fell asleep on the couch.

The next morning, two military officers who might have camped out the night before in an unmarked car drove me to the office of the Mayor. I hesitated to join them at first, but they assured me it was protocol and for my own safety.

They had me wait in a conference room and, noticing my apprehension, served me coffee and fresh baked cookies. Before I could gulp down my second sip, the Mayor walked in. As was customary, I bowed in acquiescence and then kept my head down until he spoke.

"It is of my understanding that you have returned to make a difference and have agreed to follow all government procedures and strict guidelines. May I remind you, Mr. Kootan, that if you succeed, and I hope you will, the opportunity to move up the rank will be limitless? If you fail, however, the ramifications will be severe. I know you are young; you will be not alone. All I am asking you is to be vigilant. The Queen will be incredibly happy with you, and she will even ask you to meet with her. Do you think you have the confidence and determination to change things around quickly?" She uttered.

I shook my head in agreement but that was not the right thing to do. I had been warned earlier not to speak directly to a superior in Port-Au-Prince or show disagreement even if he or she was dead wrong. Since I was not allowed to say anything, I presumed I was right in being silent until I heard the clicking sound of a gun by an officer who stood right behind my back. I took that fearfully.

"Yes, your excellence," I responded. Surprisingly, Francis Duval showed up.

The agony in my voice and my eyes sunken in fear were all there to see. There was no way to tell if she cared. I could hear her very well, though I was very much looking at the size of her exotic diamond ring, the exquisite yet expensive necklace, and, of course, the dress. Francis Duval was known to be ruthless but visionary. Dignitaries were overwhelmed by her generosity.

And when she took the time to explain her plans in detail, which rarely happened, by the way, fellow countrymen applauded her. Her private life was just that—private.

"Do you agree to obey the laws of the land?" she asked.

"Yes, your Almighty. I shall obey all the laws of the land. It will, of course, be a matter of time to learn what they are." I replied.

"Remember, I am aware of everything that goes on here and all the way to Valparaizo where you will be working. So, I will know about your progress, or the lack thereof." She said.

She turned her back and walked away. I was surely being dismissed, the weight on my chest decreased.

To me, President Francis Duval was the living Papa Zaka, the strong voodoo character. They even had some sort of resemblance, after all. But the Queen had a different religious faith. I was about to ask her about her voodoo belief…even this Owl's story. I just kept my mouth shut. I did want to jeopardize my chance.

It didn't take me long to get my official papers from the Minister of Public Works, signed a mountain of documents to the point I thought I might have given my life away, and left to return to the hotel.

It was nearly dark, so through my window I watched the falling rain and the rainbow disappearing into view. When

Briane came out of the toilet, she caught her breath and broke into a smile that sprung from an enduring pain. I stupidly thought she had pain in her leg, which was rested on the pillow, and I began to massage it. Briane suddenly harangued me.

"Do you really believe we are safe in this country? Remember just to add to the previous joke, here, the Owl does not have to pay neither for an airplane ticket nor for a visa to reach us." I supposed,

"First, I have nothing to do with this curse. I am not one of your Mom's boys. Number two, two years have gone since we have not heard anything about this Owl, obviously he is either dead or everything was a joke. So, don't worry about this son of a gun." Suddenly, Briane screeched,

"How did it all go today?" I responded,

"Everything went fine, sweetheart. I got the job." She jumped off the bed, full of joy.

"I'm so proud of you. You must have made a great impression today. So, go to hell...you, stupid Owl, I am not afraid of you anymore," shouted Briane.

I proudly stood up and shouted to the top of my lung,

"VICTORY! VICTORY! VICTORY!"

"You're really scared me to death Kootan! What's going on Cherie?"

"Indeed! For so many years I have been trying to realize just that for God. I tried to convince Kiti, that was impossible. But I had faith. Now, I am convinced I finally got you. I loved what you've just said." Briane screeched,

"If I were in this predicament, I would have done same danm thing. In fact, Cherrie, let me reaffirm you today. I quit! No more voodoo. Not even the loas. But I believe there is only one God for ever and ever...And I will forever be grateful to you and combine my strength to yours to rebuild our country in the name Jehovah God, Amen and Amen."

"Briane! I made this promise if you ever agree and convince there is no other God but Jehovah, the only one that we would rebuild Valparaizo and marry you. "Now! Would you want to marry me?"

"Yes, I do!" said Briane cheerfully.

Chapter IX

Valparaizo's Renaissance and Wedding

I called Colas and asked him if he would be interested in being my chauffeur. He happily agreed, and since he did, I was not concealing anything from him. I just did not know my way around after so many years out of the country. Not only that I needed a person of confidence, someone I could really trust. Colas fit this gap. "When do you start working?" He asked.

I showed him the paper with the date I am supposed to report to work. Evidently, the minister had not bothered looking for pen. He signed my documents with pencil which I felt very strange. Yes! I would have to report to the Corps of Engineers first thing Monday morning. And, moreover, I would have everything at my disposal, all the perks needed to start what I needed in Valparaizo zone. But everything was a fairytale, incredible if not a dream-come-true for all of us, Briane, Colas, and me.

"Don't you think it's a little bit too soon? You just got the contract." Pointed out Colas. I suspected he probably did not want to quit his other job so quick, even his family, why not, to commit himself to me so soon. I responded, "Are you on board or aren't you Colas?" I added,

"We'll manage this, I'm sure." He retorted quickly, "I am on board Kootan."

Essentially, we went through the list of the most priorities.

I dispatched him to go and get a brand-new sports utility vehicle.

The following day, we loaded the truck and checked out. I was about to foot the bill in cash when the owner greeted me and told me the government already took care of it. I was amazed how slowly Colas drove while leaving the lot. So was Briane, who seemed to have been ready for a rough ride from Port-Au-Prince to Valparaizo. A great driver always remained the greatest. Colas got us to our destination with no problem.

We did not even step the city ground; Mayor Turenne was already waiting with his own crews to welcome us. We delivered the gifts and goods we brought for him as he exchanged our room and board to us. But he could not stop shower his face throughout his outfit by seeing Briane. That was too many memories for him. Could he be this father girl father people began to wonder? Meanwhile, what was so strange was, peasants and suburban had been alarmed on our incoming. They were ready to launch some kind festivities to welcome us because our return meant a lot to them. They knew our love for the city. They had been expecting us for the longest to fulfill our promise, to change their condition.

The moment of truth just hit me hard. The transition toughened my skin. I was assigned to work on the hardest project in the North West part of the island. Every waking day, I would have to conduct and monitor land surveys for a road construction work. I was given instructions on how to proceed and tackle almost every unforeseen problem.

It was full daylight now, and my crew barricaded the hilltop. We were determining the feasibility and the expansion of the curves since this major road served all the counties in and on the outskirts of Valparaizo. We looked at our plan, tweaked it a little bit, and drew a new one instantly.

I took to exploring and overseeing everything. My duty seemed to have skyrocketed right before my eyes. I put all my energy into it, beyond exhaustion.

Suddenly, we all laughed at a man who tried to remove the barricade so his herd of goats could walk through. Even funnier, he did not dare ask us for permission. He was drunk and acted as if we were on his way. He was determined to cross the path, and no one could stop him.

I was watching this whole shenanigan unfold from afar. I was in charge, and it was time to put an end to this. This was too much, I believed, stepping forward. I was not quite sure how to approach him from behind, so I fumbled at my pocket for a pen and wrote a note to our security officer, demanding that was to be over. Effortlessly, the officer arrested the man. Come to find out, it was my cousin Rodney.

"My own blood's treatin' me like dirt." Rodney said. He smelled heavily of alcohol and tobacco. He could not stand straight or keep his eyes open. And when he did, I could see a man who was rebellious and annoying and subsequently resigned from life.

I persuaded the officer to handcuff Rodney and let him go his merry way. I knew I would undoubtedly see him again and only then I would chastise him for his antics.

A few hours later, as we were all wrapping up along the embankment where the potholes awed us more than the misty hilltop, there was a moment of relief, a sense that we were heading in the right direction. I particularly felt wise about this project. My spirit lifted.

I was disconcerted too, because now Rodney was making his way back towards us at a fast pace. Everyone was on alert. Eyes blinked at me, all my fault supposedly.

"Now what?" I shouted at Rodney.

He put down his bag slowly, opened it, and took out the fried meat and the spicy sauce. It was, he said, something to munch on.

And we did. It was delicious. We licked out fingers. Colas joked that I should hire Rodney to cook for the team. Jogging back from the park, my footsteps thumped in the hardened mud, I longed for rest. I was already halfway through my backyard and well into my garden area when I saw a dead rooster lying on top of my most blossomed flower plant. I did not think much of it. All I had to do was get rid of it.

"I just wanted you to see that." Colas said, coming from behind me.

"You could have thrown that thing away." I replied.

Colas was now more just my driver. He felt it was his duty to protect me at all costs. His livelihood depended on me. No, his meager salary could not afford his lifestyle or take care of his large family. But, as I noticed, he had been loaning money to farmers and flipping the profit.

"You see how its head is decapitated, don't you?" he asked.

"What's that supposed to mean? Someone must have thrown it here. Is that what you are insinuating?" I said forcefully.

"Don't be naïve, Kootan. Apparently, someone does not like what you are doing in this town. If you continue, that is what is going to happen to you. Get my drift?" He boasted.

At first, I thought he was bicycling elephants and ultimately resorted in mystified skulls and crossbones. He was so adamant about it and he had me thinking along the same lines.

"Last week, it was a broken glass and now this. You've got to secure this place, that's all I'm saying." He said briskly.

"I bet if you move in with me, you'll catch that person in no time." I said, straightforwardly.

And that was exactly what Colas was looking for but did not bother asking. He knew that was not going to happen—an arrangement Briane would have a fit about. And he was also aware that I held my privacy dear. How best would I handle this? I wondered since I was nervous. I just returned here, and my list of foes was growing.

"I might have to start pressuring some people around here." He said.

"Don't be stupid. I need everybody's support. They are just beginning to understand the importance of my work. They know what I am about. I'm going to need them later." I said.

"I wouldn't trust them if I were you. Anyway, I must go see a friend. What time do you need me here later?" He asked.

I told him I did not need him, and I was taking the truck. He handed me the keys and walked out through the front gate with the dead bird in a shopping bag.

I slowly drove past a cascade of trees and veered off the lush side street where Briane had told me she would be. But she was not. I checked out the address once more, I was in the right location.

As I waited for what seemed to be an eternity, my worries worsened. Now I wished I had picked her up, all things considered. My intuition was sealed when all eyes turned towards me. Negative thoughts ran quickly through my brain but eased out when Briane emerged from the back of the torn-down private home she was considering buying. Beside her was an old woman, named Shanaz, the former city hall secretary in her late seventies. She expertly managed paraphernalia with her eyes hidden beneath a hat. But everyone seemed to be in the most cheerful spirits.

"This is my fiancée." Briane said, trying vaguely to introduce us.

"How do you do, ma'am?" I said politely.

"I'm fine, young man. Tired but hanging there. You look familiar." She said, holding me by the wrist.

I did not just look familiar. As a matter of fact, that woman had known my parents well and done business with them. I listened with the keenest interest how she had fought and won a battle against the local government over eminent domain. Because of her refusal and tenacity to give up her house, the road had never been built. She had threatened the mayor at the time, Mr. Turenne.

She was known as the woman who had chased the mayor with a bamboo stick and later sought the help of a group of Mazingas to protest.

Why did she change her mind now? Well, for all the good reasons. She just heard Briane's plan for the house and she was excited about it. It was to be converted into a medical clinic.

"She's brilliant, isn't she?" Isabel said.

"She sure is. Always came up with great ideas." I replied.

"If you think so, why you don't marry her?" She asked, sticking her Pinocchio nose into something that was none of her business.

"That is the plan, ma'am. We are going to do it soon. You'll be invited, and we'll expect to see you there."

Isabel carefully cheered herself with the notion that she would make the wedding cake and assist Briane in picking up the dress.

"Can I be the flower girl, Dr. Briane?" she asked jokingly.

"Anything you want to do is fine with us." Briane replied.

I walked her back inside the house, but I was disheartened to see its conditions. It needed work, mostly on the brick walls and the electrical wires.

Positive thoughts overcame me. I saw the potential. So was Briane. What needed to turn the house into a functional medical clinic was done quickly. I sought the help of many locals and most of them came true. I had Colas driving back and forth to Port-Au-Prince for construction materials and tools. Even under the most severe pressure, they all did hard work, be it masonry or carpentry. The plumbing was a challenge unto itself. If I provided them hot meals and small allowances, they were all right. Of course, Rodney asked to be paid daily. This was sometimes twice if he caught Briane in a good mood. He was milking it, without shame. The night before the grand opening I threw a party for the crew and thanked them. I would have bought more bottles of rum and liquor had I known they would bring friends and relatives.

The clinic, it turned out, was the first woman's health center. It offered all kinds of services, from free pregnancy test to childbirth. Dr. Briane and her nursing staff were extremely busy for the next year, working long hours. The word got around rather quickly. She was once featured in the local paper. She wanted to expand the center's left wing to accommodate more beds. What did she do? She used that super smart cranium of hers to solicit funds from international relief organizations. I was skeptical about that, but she proved me wrong. She made sure Colas and I were there the day she toured the place to a group of foreign doctors and nurses, mostly New Yorkers. I was even dumbfounded when she got a check for the expansion right on the spot and got them to pledge more than what she had planned. Two white nurses who were so impressed by Briane's determination and her effective plan decided to stay.

Medical equipment and devices were either donated or bought cheaply. Chairs, conference tables, and desks were designed and built by a master carpenter, who volunteered his skill sets and went on to say he did it in memory of Briane's mother, Kitibel.

Folks she did not know gave her ceiling fans, light bulbs, and switches in abundance.

Boxes of hygienic products, syringes, and first-aid kits filled one large room. I installed a power generator as the main source of electricity and ran the water from the nearby creek, all in reliability.

There was so much to do with the local women. Briane also knew the center would, through word of mouth and outreach programs, soon be serving other counties. She was, naturally, ahead of the game. And then the result came in. Women were having healthy pregnancy and lifestyle. That much was obvious.

The infant mortality rate lowered significantly. And that too was evident.

Briane became a star, almost overnight. I was proud of my fiancée.

It was the kind of pride that came with a double meaning. She was a delightful companion, traveled across the city, and became quite an expert on women's health issues. She established herself rather quickly. She had no reproach. None whatsoever.

I felt she was leaving me behind, and that whatever she did afterwards I should be part of. And so, with classic optimism and a knack to outperform Briane, I began to work longer hours on the most important projects. Hardly a day seemed to pass—only then was it time to get permission to build a bridge. With three detailed sketches lying on the desk, I tried to persuade my boss that the plan was in fact doable and that would save us time and money. He welcomed my interest, argued over minor points in design but agreed on the cost estimate.

"I'm sorry to say we don't have the money to build that bridge." He said.

"I know but you can send this plan to the proper authority in Port-au-Prince and see what comes of it. What you got to lose?"

I said, convincingly.

"I could get fired if the minister of Public Works doesn't like the idea. My reputation would be on the line if I could not raise the money or finish the project on time. Besides, let me share this with you, Mr. Kootan. I am not here to stay. Once the last project's done in a few weeks or so, I am going to return home. I'm sick of this town." He replied.

He led me through the smooth-swinging metal door into a dark room and showed me leftover construction materials, such as steel beams and cement. What he did not say was that I could use those if I needed to, but he wanted no part of it.

The following month, he received the transfer he had requested and was thrilled to be leaving town. He wished me luck and said he would be back occasionally to offer his opinion and expertise if I ever got lucky to push my plan through the red tape and I did.

There was a consensus among all engineers and local people that the bridge was needed and that, among other important things, the counties would be flourishing. I gathered enough support and praise but there was one problem—one that reached deep inside my guts. The government had no money to fund my project, so it was now considered dreadfully dead.

At the beginning of July, I announced I was going to build the bridge. I was more than ready after I had convinced many business folks to give a small donation and thus solicited manpower from the Mazingas.

While construction was underway, I fulfilled many tasks on and out of the site. I was the first to be there in the morning and the last to leave. I was strict and adamant about everything, but I also suspected some workers were stealing bags of cement.

Dr. Briane would come by during lunch breaks not only to force me to eat but also to talk about our wedding plan in depth. Once a month, she would bring along her nursing staff to vaccinate and hand out free condoms to the laborers right then and there.

Along the way I tweaked the design, and that helped me finish the bridge faster. Right on time, too, since there was a growing impatience among the people involved.

The bridge, which was named after former mayor Turenne, was erected, and approved to be of use immediately. That, in and of itself, ended the fear among citizens to travel across counties.

We celebrated, drank, ate, and kidded around. I did it. In fact, we all did it. Thanks to my tenacity, no one would ever die crossing the river again.

I also kept the momentum going. I assembled a small crew I could trust and, in less than a month, I had the cathedral's floor restored and all cracks on the bricklayer repaired.

I had success in concealing that small project from Dr. Briane, but she found out on the day of our wedding. Who could have told her? I figured it was, or had to be, the gossipy old woman friend of hers.

We both were shocked at the wedding ceremony. We had invited a handful of relatives and friends and made arrangement accordingly, but the cathedral was full. All the men who worked on my projects were present and, moreover, they brought their women along. There was cheer when I said, "I do" and then kissed the bride. The parade had just begun throughout Valparaizo streets.

The car stood idling in front of the church longer than usual. Time seemed interminably slow. The driver, who failed to remember he was hired for the day, looked impatient and worrisome. Whatever he was thinking or mulling over was quickly shun aside as Briane and I hopped in.

He congratulated us, while keeping his eyes on the steering wheel.

"You're now officially husband and wife."

Sure, we were the newlyweds and would soon be a powerful and respectable couple. There was no doubt with that, and we were hoping the perks would be significant and enhance our lifestyle.

This was meant to be the beginning of a new life.

When we arrived at the reception, Briane invited our driver to come in and mellow with the ladies in attendance. He felt honored and offered to help with the train of her dress.

There were far more guests here, even those I had not sent invitations to. They came because they felt they had to. And, make no mistake about that, they would not pass on delicious Creole cuisine and free drinks either. This, too, turned out to be an informal gathering among corrupt politicians, ill-advised appointed officials, and courageous laymen. Their gifts, most in petty cash, added comfort. I decided I would listen to their demands later.

Meanwhile, Briane seemed occupied with her well-groomed friends—most were in the medical field and single. The glow in Briane's face was radiant. Something they all thought was sincere.

This reception seemed to take forever, and understandably, I wished it would now end. I took notice of the vespers and toadies who sat still and talked about business deals and what not. If I had not complained about the long hours at the ceremony, I was inclined to do so now, knowing full well my insistence would be taken as inconsiderate and gullible.

I was exhausted beyond belief. I spilled my glass of champagne on a tablecloth, but I thought nothing of it. I felt sorry for my wife, having walked around on high heels. But the anticipation what loomed ahead kept me going. She whispered in my ears, something to that effect.

"Is there a way we can get out of here without being noticed?"

"I'm sure there is. Wait here and I'll ask the driver to meet us outside."

"I sent him home to drop the gift packages," she said in a sobbing tone. "It's been a while. Have you seen him around?"

"As a matter of fact, I haven't. If I were you, I would not worry about it. He should be here any minute. As soon he does, we'll leave quietly."

And so, we did. We were in the backseat, all snuggling and relaxing, when the driver reminded us that the station was miles away and the last bus would leave on time. Speeding through hills and lushes was now becoming quite refreshing. The breezy air meant the autumn was here.

"Let me give you young married couple a piece of advice," he stammered, waiting for a reaction. "If you trust one another most of the time, you would forever be inseparable."

"We will forever remember that." I said.

"Have you ever been married?" Briane asked.

"Three times. And I got divorced three times too. Why? I am sure you want to know why, and I will tell you. Lack of trust."

"You didn't trust any of them, did you?" I asked.

"On the contrary, they didn't trust me. Jealousy made them blind. Look, driving is what I have been doing to maintain. I am out there day and night. If a woman believes I am cheating on her, that is her issue to deal with, not mine."

He got a convincing point, a telltale with no happy ending. I shared his views, though I would not dare say so.

"They all three couldn't be possibly wrong. Don't you think?" Briane asked.

He went on to explain the type of women he had been dealing with—the type who would indeed not hesitate to roll him onto the ground like a sack of flour. Maybe it was his attitude that oftentimes got him into hot water or his sinister grudge that induced him to go insane. Whatever the case may have been, he seemed to be too eager to claim innocence.

"None of my ex-wives knew how to save a penny. I mean—even a penny."

"You can't save what you don't have," Briane bellowed.

"Come on. Save something, for Christ's sake! You never know when there's gonna be a case of an emergency. Besides, things are getting tighter. I do not make as much money as I used to. So, when I give her something, she'd better manage it well."

I took in a deep breath and shifted in my seat uneasily, wondering if we were going in opposite direction. He was not endangering us but was not too allowing us to be relaxed. The bumpy ride did not make things smoother either.

"You two have no idea what I'm talking about because you have jobs. You got paychecks coming in. I don't."

"We got large bills to pay. Did you think of that?" I said.

His surprise was clearly false. His resentment was too much to bear. His world was different than mine, I reminded him bluntly, but what to make of it?

"I hope you two have fun," he said as he pulled up near the curve.

Briane implored that I should give him a wad of cash, much more than I had promised. I felt I was being conned, but I obeyed her request, for the sake of having a peace of mind.

This was, after all, the most joyous day of our lives. If Briane or I had anticipated a prolonged fun ride, we would have been wrong. The bus we got on en route to the capital smelled terribly yucky and almost every passenger was half-asleep.

It was starkly dark, night owls noticeably sprawling from afar. We soon reached a town called L'Esther where people used to grow rice in abundance. That whole rice farming was now almost gone, and the land looked as torrid and uncared for. Also gone were the livestock and the tall trees. Shameful, it was indeed.

We crossed a small bridge if you could call it that. I had never seen a bridge so small and creaky. I had a foreboding feeling the builders had died long ago and there was no one qualified to maintain it. It looked as though the devil must have put his spell on it. It was torture and horrific. Now it was beyond repair, a new one would have to be built. The locals knew and demanded that to be done, but, alas, their voices were not heard.

"This could be a good assignment for you, my dear," Briane whispered frantically. I would have liked that if the opportunity were laid at my door. I was certain that I would have done a good job, and my popularity skyrocketing.

"Right now, the only assignment worth my time is you," I said flatteringly.

"Tough, isn't it?"

"I wouldn't say that. At least, not yet."

"Get used to it, sweetheart. I'm not about to change course."

"I wouldn't want you to, Briane. I love you just the way you are."

"I hope to hear you say that when I'm ninety years old."

"By then, you'll be generous enough to forgive me and also forget that you once asked."

At this point, I raised my eyes and saw the crooked "Welcome to Port-Au-Prince's sign."

That sign was old and looked more like the pigeons' nest. She could care less. All she anticipated to do now was to get to the hotel and called it a day.

We had indeed reserved a room at Titanik Hotel, one of the most elegant. It was nothing like Pierre, Palace, Woldoff Astoria hotel of New York City, but it was on a great location and offered great panorama and tranquility. We also had chosen that hotel for a slew of other reasons—the chief one being far away from my kinfolks.

None of us had been there before, though we had heard about how great the service was and how fantastic the décor was. We had to find out for ourselves.

Upon our arrival, the girl at the concierge who was filing her nails and answering phone calls greeted us politely in French but switched to Creole as she handed us the room key. It was that fast, she had no qualm about that. I also noticed she was a bit mesmerized by the way Briane looked. Was it the size of Briane's diamond ring or her whole ensemble?

As I glanced on the schedule, I overheard my favorite song playing softly in the background and I frowned, trying to remember the singer's name. I was dreamy and excited all the way. Briane looked away and came up with the right name.

"It's Lonald Richard, sweetheart."

"I think you're right. Why didn't I think so?"

"Shortly, we shall be on her way for the big thing."

"Will you please share what's that big thing."

"I surely will Baby" I responded.

"THE HONEY MOON!"

We hugged each other and proceeded to Titanic's hotel.

CHAPTER X

Prophecy Comes True

Mother Nature shattered all the activities regardless throughout the city at large. At that hour, people had been ready to inhale the last breath of a tormented day. What would be next, the uncertainty? Who knows?

The mansaras (street vendors) are yet to figure out what to do because sooner the streets would be filled up of consumers and commodities. Suddenly, yelled some voice in unison, "Look up the sky?" They quickly unfolded their tacky veil over their possessions, their only means of survival. A stumbling noise amplified the atmosphere while a murky cloud expanded over the city. The echo resumed so far away from the city outskirts and reverberated all around the city. And people so traumatized and alleged,

"Can this be the thunderstorm that triggered this turbulence?"

"No! It had not rained for many months, the verdures began to fade away; the dryness probably provoked such turbulence," one Hougan said and broke out by fear.

"We experienced an act of God. We're about to be blessed," a preacher yelled.

Startlingly, people looked for undercover.

Suddenly, the same repeated once again, this time with problematic. The religious institutions regardless began to fill up of people to implore God of Heaven for forgiveness, "We are not all sinners…God please have mercy on us!" yelled the Christians. But the hougans, mambos, kanzos, and Honsys invoked instead, "Danballa, Papa Legba, Erzuly, Agwee…where are you?

All over, every which where, it was the same. The national palace, police station, and Supreme Court, you name it were no different. They are packed up with street vendors seeking for undercover.

Briane and I were not exceptional. Even though we came to Titanic Hotel for our honeymoon, we felt we were nothing special, just the ordinary Haitians struggling for protection and forgiveness. But if Briane was looking for humility, she sure found tons of it in my voice. I blamed it on my poor memory and, when that did not fare well, I convinced myself I had been away for too long. It was indeed pitiful that I could not sing a song along. I loved to chant the soul music in similar circumstances to elevate our soul and encourage. So, I buried my face in what appeared to be an event schedule for my honeymoon.

At first, I doubted we could partake in all, but I would let Briane decide which event to attend. Something was supposed to be happening every half-hour, apparently without intermission. It hurt my eyes, looking at it. As it seemed, we would have to be here and there, up, and down, and mingle with mostly foreigners. Could this be real, and did it mean anything? The event planner, I said to myself, must have been on drugs or something.

I did not know what Briane thought of it, but I was not overwhelmingly happy about that sort of arrangement. All I wanted to do at this point was to go to our room and gulp down a shot of Babancourt (a famous Haitian's rhum). And that was what I did as soon as we entered the room.

I plopped on the sofa, but the cushion bounced me back. It was not until I looked out the window that I realized we sure did not get the room we had requested. We thought we had reserved a room with a panoramic view of the city. They must have wronged us. There was something dismal and humiliating in all this deprivation.

"I'm going back downstairs to talk to the manager. I can't believe this." I said.

"It might be too late to make a fuss about it. Besides, we will not be here for long."

"I hate surprises. I really do."

I walked rapidly with long strides, and she followed me all the way to the door.

"Can't you wait until the morning?" she asked.

"I sure can. But I am pissed because we need to unpack. Shuttling from one room to another is not my idea of joy."

"I couldn't have agreed with you more."

"This is fine. We don't live here, nor we do have plans to."

Briane did not care much. Evidently restless and sobbing, she longed for a quiet moment. She sat on the chair and, while she was about to take her shoes off, I peeked through the windows yet again. I was contemplating nature on the outside and beauty on the inside. In my unfettered mind, I wished I could have blended them together. And I did. I just realized how profoundly I knew her and how fascinating it was that I already grew accustomed to her mannerisms. She was destined to be my significant other half.

When she was sad, which rarely happened, I felt I should jump on the person who made her feel sad like a spider monkey jacked up on a Bwa Cochon (local rhum). I was in love, so I inanely concealed my being possessive. Moreover, when she was feeling blue due to family reminiscence or stress from work, I took it upon myself to dislodge whatever was choking her.

We were so intimately close we could finish each other's sentences. However, right at this minute, I was not thinking about making a speech. My body was telling me to do something else, something I had long craved for. I slid across the room, dancing. My feet moved like an ostrich and my head swiveled like a chicken.

I hugged her tight and, in so doing, I felt her nipples hardening. She howled smoothly, and I knew she was plotting something I would have to be involved in.

"You act like you're…" she mumbled.

"The captain of the ship." I added.

"Yes, that's right."

"In all honesty, I thought I was."

"Of course, you are. But you must know that sometimes the captain can be taken hostage. What will you do then?"

"I don't know what I will do. But one thing I am certain of, I will comply with any request just to save the ship."

"What if it were sinking?"

"I would be the first one to drown. It's my ship, remember."

She pushed me on the bed and lay on top of me. I felt powerless but I sure enjoyed her touch. And, no doubt, she enjoyed mine all night long until we fell asleep.

The next morning, I ordered breakfast without consulting her. She was still in bed, half-awake and exhausted. We had made plans to meet Colas and his family for lunch but now I knew that was not going to happen.

I fell into her arms and, caressing her neck I slowly kissed her on the lips and disrobed her. When she pressed her hands on her temple in ecstasy, I knew I had to stop.

"I feel a tad feverish. I need to take some pills." She said, on the way to the bathroom.

"Wait. Let me take your temperature and see how high it is."

I pleaded, as though to show concern.

She was hot as a burning charcoal, jumping up and trembling all over. I wrongly thought she was pregnant, but I wished I had been right. She was, after all, in her early thirties and we both said we wanted to have kids. We hoped a baby would bring us even much closer and we would be proud parents. We understood the frustrations and challenges lurking ahead, but we paved the way to tackle them with fervor.

I remembered we once had this discussion over dinner.

She had lamented she would prefer a girl first and I nonchalantly naïve, had agreed.

"Will you please call downstairs and ask if they have some oil?" She inquired.

Oh my God! I knew she was referring to the popular Haiti's oil namely (Maskreti). We had used it before, so we could authoritatively talk about its effectiveness. This hotel would not have it around, I was sure of that.

I made up my mind to go look for it. She was happy I was going too.

"Be careful."

"You might want to take a nap while I'm gone."

"I will be lying right here and watch my favorite TV program. I will be waiting for you just like you like me to. So, if I were you, I would try to hurry back."

"I wouldn't want to leave you here alone. I love you." She cackled and, clearing her throat, said sarcastically.

"Can you make the wind blow?"

It was her way of telling me to leave in a hurry and stop playing God.

Taking long strides down the narrow corridor, I was on the phone with my boss who clearly preferred to talk about my honeymoon than work. Before I could reach the main street, I stumbled upon a street vendor from whom I purchased a half-pint of oil. There was no room for negotiation. She charged me extra simply because I looked like a tourist.

As I made my way back to the hotel, I heard a loud explosion. I did not know if it was emanating from the sky or below the surface. The second explosion had me shaken in my boots and peed my pants. I was not daydreaming nor hallucinating. I felt I was sinking in and the whole city weighted on my shoulder. This was real.

This was a goddamn earthquake.

I looked up and saw nothing but debris flying all over the place. Titanic Hotel took a big hit; the whole front tumbled down.

The damage was far less substantial in the back. Still in shock but hopeful, I began to remove rubbles with my bare hands and screamed my lungs out, while searching for my wife.

Did Briane survive or die? I had to find that out on my own.

On my knees, I invoked the names of Jesus Christ and shook my head as I did. I prayed, in fact, to God, the Almighty. My speech was inaudible and tears glistening in my eyes. Yet I refused to believe she was forever gone. No way. I had fate. I was digging as fast I could. And the more I did, the worse I let things got. There were little bits of audible gurgle underneath the rubble coming from teenagers and younger. Everything on the near side of the hotel was quickly melted into a dark, billowing mass. Only the aftershocks could be felt.

What I saw was indescribably gruesome. And in this stifling heat, I would be foolish to think help was on the way.

Chaos reigned in with peculiar distinctness. Confusion was settling in as the city experienced aftershocks—of which there were plenty. Luckily, some of the guests who had occupied the front side were still alive and well, but they were too busy searching for their loved ones.

My hands were bleeding but that did not prevent me from tossing aside sharp objects and remains of concrete.

After many ensuing hours, I began to contemplate that I would have to do something drastic, something strictly out of the ordinary. Or else, I would be a widow. But what exactly was I to do? I was in the line of duty, there was no getting around it.

In the aftermath, things worsened even more. I was told that the quake had hit the city and all other places on a scale of seven-point-zero and did all those damages within seconds.

An inventory would later reveal how catastrophic the quake was. The death toll was astronomical, and the financial loss was estimated to be over billions of dollars.

It was reported that well over two hundred thousand people might have died and thousands of private homes and commercial buildings were severely hampered. A few landmarks were irreparably damaged, particularly the infamous Roman Catholic cathedral.

I had been there before on numerous occasions and stunned by its beauty and its structural composition. Now to hear that it was gone could not escape my memory.

It was a sigh of relief to learn no one died inside the cathedral. The National Palace, built during the Occupation, was hard hit but everyone who was there at the time suffered bruises. There was no electricity. It appears the power grid had ceased to function, and the lampposts knocked down. Everyone was frightened.

Things went from bad to worse when the main state prison collapsed, and prisoners of all stripes escaped. Those same ex-convicts began to loot. There were no police officers around to stop them either. Life was no longer a pleasure but a duty. Death itself became a way of life.

Even the elected and appointed officials were nowhere to be found.

At that point, the world leaders sent cables to show sympathy. That effort was well-received but stopped short of addressing the main concern. The scores of poor folks had to be rescued, fed, and sheltered.

Of all the things that I witnessed, only one did not irritate me, the mere presence of a foreign aid, when the first foreign convoy arrived, probably the invaders that the Haitians army had kicked out from Islands many decades ago. Anyhow, the relief effort was very welcome by Francis Duval. For once, politics and diplomatic demagoguery were put aside. Racism and indifference took a backseat. I assisted that for the first in my lifetime. The media participated as reporters and rescuers in the ordeal. I was somewhat relieved and gained some incentives to live again when I saw an edgy group of volunteers joined in and began to remove the rubbles by their bare hands. How amazing and efficient that was!

As time went by and folks worked tirelessly, there was a glimmer of hope that some of those buried under the rubbles were still breathing and would ultimately be rescued.

Standing over a gargantuan pile, I kept telling a few volunteers that my wife might be stranded near here and I needed their help.

They heard my plea. We went to work and, lo and behold, Briane was rescued alive three days later. She could barely open her eyes and calling out my name. I uttered,

"Thank you, Lord."

There was cheer among us – most notably me. I thanked everyone in more ways than one. I decided I would take it from there.

Rescuing Briane was one thing but taking her to a hospital for treatment became the stuff of nightmares for me. As it was, all the two main hospitals in the city were shut down if not also perished in the trial. What would I do next?

She was taken to a nearby military ship where medical personnel stationed. When I got there, I pronounced, "We will never get out here." This medical personal was the only facility that was opened. Briane was immediately being treated. The bleeding stopped, the bruises banded over, and the left arm put on a sling. Then I said.

"Now, we'll need to find out how to get back home quickly."

"No, not just like that, I suppose, I need to get discharged before I go home," said Briane.

I confronted her Physician. "Is Briane ready to leave here?"

"Absolutely! Despite the agony that she went through, she looks fine to me."

But Briane was not impressed at all. She was concerned about the shortage of doctors and scores of patients who needed care like her. Anyhow, she said. "Doctor! This country is indebted to you. And in the name of Haitian people, I thank you for all you do for us."

We dismissed the hospital and proceeded to the Bus station.

"What exactly took place at Titanic?" She asked innocently in our way there.

She continued. "I don't know how best to describe that tragedy. In short, the hotel fell, and I got stuck. Since I was asleep, I don't remember anything."

Inconceivable! "You didn't feel the quake at all? Didn't you hear the explosions?"

"All I can remember is I was in a long, profound dream. That was about my mom threatening to whoop my butt if I did not take my brothers to school. Oh Gosh, she was horrible and mean, totally out of character, I must say." Then, Briane stopped.

"How bad is it in Valparaizo? Do you know? I am really thinking about these poor people. They are so vulnerable. They have nothing to rely on in a situation like that."

"I don't know. I tried to call a few people but to no avail."

"Is our house damaged?"

"We'll soon find out. See, we've got to get back home rather quickly."

Unfortunately, there was no Bus Station either. It was halted since the earthquake and no sign it would soon be improved.

Turene Jr. had courageously dispatched a bid delegation to Port-au-Prince, ostensibly looking for us. If we had needed to be rescued from the rubbles, they would help in doing so. I did not know what Briane was thinking, I was in shock when I saw this delegation headed by Colas.

No one wanted to talk about the tragedy that kidnapped the soul of the nation. Colas uttered. "Good morning guys. Are you okay?"

The others followed up, "Good morning."

I finally grabbed my head. "You don't know what ordeal we went through."

"Of course, we sure know, but God is good," said the driver.

We immediately hit the road. We should avoid bad weather and the aftermath of the Earthquake. We stay there quietly for three hours while the driver drove carefully, Colas suggested. "Kootan! I know what you went through but, let us pretend it did not ever happen. Let us crack some jokes."

"That's not bad," said the driver. Everyone listened attentively.

"Do you remember when we used to play soccer after school? We could not find any ball, but we did it anyway. We made our balls with socks, four to six pairs for a good one. We dropped our book bags on the dusty, unpaved streets. Each player had to spare his socks. By the time we finished, we would tear all of them. We used to be punished severely for it. Remember Kootan?" Everyone tried extremely hard not to smile.

"Kootan! I found it extremely hard to believe that Kitibel was dating the mayor. He used to visit her every night. He would sit on a bench next to her. They would share the same plate of griot and tassot (fried pork and goat meat) with Haitian's five stars babancourt." Briane did not bulge.

Colas continued. "His children were so rich and sophisticated, and they used to live in the best part of the city. They would drive expensive vehicles while we walked."

Briane looked at him. "Colas hold your horse! For the record, Turenne Sr. maintained only a business relationship with my mother. But I suspect there was a secret between them. Maybe the mayor used to visit Isabel, Perpetua, and Carolle as well. Woman was so defenseless at the time. Why not! That was the way of life at the time. Man holds all the political power and woman nothing." "Absolutely," Kootan said.

"It is absurd," added Colas. Now, I imagined something unheard of to dismiss this argument.

"Who is presently our mayor Colas? Turenne Jr., right?"

"Who was his father?"

"Mayor Turenne."

"What about you? What do you do for a living?" "Driving a cab," Colas said.

"And your father…what did he do for a living?"

"Carpentry," Colas said.

"This means that the rich will always keep this trend until we do something about it. And that is why I returned home to change the situation after living abroad for so many years. And I hope you are not offended Colas?" Kootan said.

"Now, I feel embarrassed. I should have made more effort in life. What a loser I turned out to be! You and I had the same vested interests," shouted Colas.

"No bitterness Kootan! We are not just friends, we are family. I'll never hold grudges against you." "Fine," said Kootan. What a task!

Now, Briane talked about her plan to assist the needy with medical care in Valparaizo. And I said I would continue doing that too until other serious projects came along. That was all we could do. "Life goes on." But what we found Kootan said very strange was that Turenne Jr. would not take any chance. He not only prepared for "Victory" but also, funeral arrangements for us in case we did not return from the earthquake ordeal.

Valparaizo's entry point was fully decorated with signs posted.

Every palm and coconut tree, lamppost, and homes carried these words.

"Welcome, Kootan and Briane! We love you! We wish you well!"

Surprisingly, we hit the entry point. Under the tight security, a new delegation escorted us to the City Hall. The mayor proudly handed us the city's humongous key and gave us the bad news. Then he said,

"Misfortune brought you back. But you two have a lot to do for the city. This is your town, your people, your world. Welcome home."

Three days had passed, we frankly thought all had been quintessentially over. Even Mayor Turene Jr., had invited us for dinner at one of the best restaurants that the city had which happened to be a five-star restaurant previously owned by Kitibel. Scores of officials and prominent guests were invited but more outrage repeated aftermath of the earthquake.

As soon as Briane worked in, she exclaimed, "This place has been so familiar to me, Cherrie!" which provoked me to bellow,

"What are you going to do Baby? Are you going to reclaim it?" Briane ignored me and yelled, "Go to Hell Mr. the Owl!"

Ironically, I grumbled, "How do you know this Owl was not female?" We both laughed about it and proceeded to the dining room for a great meal.

Unfortunately, as soon as we sat down, the TV screen was already in place to entertain the invitees. It seemed they had been ready to enjoy a stunning dinner a la carte of the day, but we preferred to relax instead. This memory happened to dominate our way of life, the earthquake's aftermath. Briane had used Zombi's story to cope with it. I personally had my own experience. I was so young at the time at Valparaizo when a hougan had turned one of my friends namely Wilfrid to a Zombie. Nowadays, we must deal with Alanfer, a career criminal, Lucifer in person.

In fact, he had moved to the south side of Hispaniola to conceal his affair. Alanfer had become deeply involved in the trade of buying and selling zombies (reviving dead people after being pronounced dead), and he had many of those in his possession to be returned before getting caught. The earthquake had turned everything upside down. All secrets would be revealed including the zombies.

Alanfer really thought the tremor meant Amagedon, the return of Jesus Christ on earth. So, he decided not to get involved in this stuff anymore, but what about the government? He risked spending time in jail or be killed in Fort Dimanche. He said perhaps sooner or later if Jesus did not make him pay retributions for the victims, the government would; and to avoid this quandary, he sooner broadcasted,

"My name is Alanfer. I reside at 1 Dumasais St., Kenskoff. If you had lost the following family members about some decades ago, I urge you to come and get them."

He stated the zombies' names one by one, but one happened to be Kitibel's. Briane, who was having dinner at the time, fall down and remained speechless. Paramedics came and did all they could, unfortunately, Briane, too, Did Not Survive.

Glossary

Location	
New York City	North American City
Alkebulan	Africa
Hispaniola:	An Island
Haiti	A nation on the Western side of Hispaniola
Port-au-Prince	the capital of Haiti
Valparaizo	A major city of Haiti
Penitencier National	A Jail in Haiti
Dominican Republic	A nation on the eastern side of Hispaniola
Santo Domingo	Capital of Dominican Republic
Olantambo	A major city of Haiti
Valparaizo	A major city of Haiti
<u>Loa</u>	Voodoo spirit
Ezili Danto	Female Voodoo spirit
Ezili Freda	Female Voodoo spirit
Gede	A high-caliber spirit
Papa Legba	Strong male Voodoo spirit
Dambala	Spirit that takes the form of a snake

Ayida Wedo	Female; Dambala's wife
Ogou Feray	Strong male spirit

Special Kreyol Terms (in alphabetical order)

grio	Deep-fried or grilled pork
kleren	A 100% proof rum
kanzo	Voodoo's early initiation
laissez-passer	Legal Permit
latrine	A communal outhouse
makome	Related by way of godmother
manyok	A woody shrub cropped in tropical regions
mazenga	A farmer's custom; A rally to sing and dance
monkompe	Related by way of godfather
potomitan	A center pole used as the loas' gateway
rara	A type of roots musical ensemble
sak pase	What is up?
taso kabrit	Deep-fried or grilled fowl meat
tetbobech	an oily lamp
tone boule-m or tone kraze-m	I swear to God
Toutoubef	A whip
Grenadie a lasso	Forward
Nan pwen Manman!	No Mom!
Nan pwen Papa	No Dad!
Sak mouri zafe ayo	It is Okay to di Swear to God
Sak pass	Wassup

www.ingramcontent.com/pod-product-compliance
Lightning Source LLC
LaVergne TN
LVHW091545060526
838200LV00036B/718